"What are you hiding, Ellie?"

"What makes you think I'm hiding something?" Ellie busied herself pouring the hot water into a mug.

"I get the feeling there's something in your past you don't like to talk about," Colt murmured.

"I didn't know full disclosure about all details of my life was necessary for me to get this job. Your grandmother seems satisfied."

He dipped his head in a curt nod. "Winnie is a great judge of character."

Meaning he had his doubts?

One of the reasons she liked being a bodyguard was that she could blend into the background. She kept a lock on her past—a past she didn't want to take out and reexamine.

"If you must know, the short version of my life so far is—"

"That's okay—I'm sorry. I didn't mean to bring up something painful."

"What did you mean?"

"To make sure Winnie was in good hands."

She stared into his light blue eyes. "She's in good hands. When I do a job, I do it one hundred percent."

Margaret Daley, an award-winning author of ninety books (five million sold worldwide), has been married for over forty years and is a firm believer in romance and love. When she isn't traveling, she's writing love stories, often with a suspense thread, and corralling her three cats, who think they rule her household. To find out more about Margaret, visit her website at margaretdaley.com.

Christmas Stalking

Margaret Daley

HARLEQUIN® LOVE INSPIRED® SUSPENSE

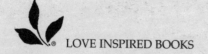

LOVE INSPIRED BOOKS

Recycling programs
for this product may
not exist in your area.

ISBN-13: 978-1-335-19851-8

Christmas Stalking

www.Harlequin.com

Printed in U.S.A.

For if ye forgive men their trespasses,
your heavenly Father will also forgive you.
—*Matthew 6:14*

To Shaun and Kim, my son and daughter-in-law

Chapter One

In the dark, Ellie St. James scanned the mountainous terrain out her bedroom window at her new client's home in Colorado, checking the shadows for any sign of trouble before she went to sleep. The large two-story house of redwood and glass blended in well with the rugged landscape seven thousand feet above sea level. Any other time she would appreciate the beauty, but she was here to protect Mrs. Rachel Winfield.

A faint sound punched through her musing. She whirled away from the window and snatched her gun off the bedside table a few feet from her. Fitting the weapon into her right palm and finding its weight comforting, she crept toward her door and eased it open to listen. None of the guard dogs were barking. Maybe she'd imagined the noise.

A creak, like a floorboard being stepped on,

drifted up the stairs. Someone was ascending to the second floor. She and her employer were the only ones in the main house. She glanced at Mrs. Winfield's door two down from hers and noticed it was closed. Her client kept it that way only when she was in her bedroom.

So who was on the stairs? Had someone gotten past the dogs outside and the security system? And did that someone not care that he was being heard coming up the steps? Because he didn't intend to leave any witnesses?

The latest threat against Mrs. Winfield urged her into action. She slipped out of her room and into the shadows of the long hallway that led to the staircase. Having memorized all the floorboards that squeaked, Ellie avoided the left side of the corridor as she snuck forward—past Mrs. Winfield's door.

Another sound echoed through the hall. Whoever was on the steps was at the top. She increased her speed, probing every dark recess around her for any other persons. Near the wooden railing of the balcony that overlooked the front entrance, she found the light switch, planted her bare feet a foot apart, preparing herself to confront the intruder, and then flipped on the hall light.

Even though she expected the bright illumination, her eyes needed a few seconds to adjust to it. The large man before her lifted his hand to shield his eyes from the glare. Which gave Ellie the advantage.

"Don't move," she said in her toughest voice, a husky resonance she often used to her advantage.

The stranger dropped his hand to his side, his gray-blue eyes drilling into her then fixing on her Wilson combat aimed at his chest. Anger washed all surprise from his expression. "Who are you?" The question came out in a deep, booming voice, all the fury in his features reflected in it.

"You don't get to ask the questions. Who are—"

The click of the door opening to Mrs. Winfield's bedroom slightly behind and to the left of Ellie halted her words as she shifted her attention for an instant to make sure the man didn't have an accomplice already with her client.

"Winnie, get back," the intruder yelled.

By the time Ellie's gaze reconnected with the man, he was charging toward her. She had less than a second to decide what to do. The use of her client's nickname caused Ellie to hesitate. In that moment the stranger barreled into her, slamming her into the hardwood floor. The impact jolted her, knocking the Wilson Combat from her hand. The thud of her weapon hitting the floor behind her barely registered as she lay pinned beneath two hundred pounds of solid muscle. Pressed into her, the man robbed her of a decent breath.

Her training flooded her with extra adrenaline. Before he could capture her arms, she brought them up and struck him on the sides of his head. His light-colored gaze widened at the blow. She latched onto his face, going for his eyes with her thumbs.

"Miss St. James, stop!" Mrs. Winfield's high-pitched voice cut into the battle between Ellie and her attacker.

The man shifted and clasped her wrists in a bone-crushing grip.

Ellie swung her attention from the brute on top of her to her employer standing over them with Ellie's gun in her quivering hand. Pointed at her!

"He's my grandson," Mrs. Winfield said. "Colt, get up. She can hardly breathe."

The man rolled off her, shaking his head as though his ears rang. After her attack they probably did.

Sitting up, he stared at his grandmother who still held the weapon. "Please give me the gun, Winnie." His soft, calm words, interspersed with heavy pants, contradicted his earlier authoritative tone.

Ellie gulped in oxygen-rich breaths while

he pushed to his feet and gently removed the weapon from Mrs. Winfield's hand. He dwarfed his petite grandmother by over a foot.

With her gun in his grasp, he stood next to her client and glared down at Ellie. "Now I would like an answer. Who are you?" Anger still coated each word.

She slowly rose from the floor. "Ellie St. James."

He put his arm around his grandmother, who stood there trembling, staring at Ellie as though she was trying to understand what had just happened. "What are you doing here, Miss St. James?" he asked.

With a shake of her head, Mrs. Winfield blinked then peered up at her grandson. "She's my new assistant."

"What in the world are you doing carrying a gun?"

His question thundered through the air, none of the gentle tone he'd used with his grandmother evident. He glared at her, his sharp gaze intent on Ellie's face. Although he'd lowered the gun, Ellie didn't think it would take much for him to aim it again. Fury was etched into his hard-planed face.

"My dear, why *do* you have a gun?"

Mrs. Winfield's light, musical voice finally pulled Ellie's attention from the man. Her employer had regained her regal bearing, her hands clasped together in front of her to control their trembling.

"I've lived alone for so long in a big city I've always had a gun for protection," Ellie finally answered.

Although Mrs. Winfield was her client—the person she'd been assigned to guard—the older woman didn't know it. Her lawyer and second-in-charge at Glamour Sensations, Harold Jefferson, had hired Guardians, Inc., to protect her. Ellie was undercover, posing as her new assistant. Her cover had her growing up in Chicago—the south side—and still living there. But in reality, at the first opportunity she'd had she'd hightailed it out of Chicago and enlisted in the army. When she'd left the military, she hadn't gone back home but instead she'd gone to Dallas to work for Guardians, Inc., and Kyra Morgan—now Kyra Hunt.

"You don't need a weapon now. This isn't a big city. I have security around the estate. You're safe. I prefer you do something with that gun. I don't like weapons." A gentle smile on her face, Mrs. Winfield moved toward her as though she were placating a gun-toting woman gone crazy.

Ellie didn't trust anyone's security enough to give up her gun, but she bit the inside of her cheeks to keep from voicing that thought. She would need to call Mr. Jefferson and see how he wanted to proceed. Ellie had wanted to tell Mrs. Winfield that her life was in danger, but he'd refused. Now something would need to give here.

"I'll take care of it, Winnie. I'll lock it in the safe until she can remove it from here." The grandson checked the Wilson Combat, slipped out the ammo clip and ejected the bullet in the chamber, then began to turn away.

"Wait. You can't—"

He peered over his shoulder, one brow arching. "I'm sure my grandmother will agree that this will have to be a condition of your continual employment. If I had any say in it, I'd send you packing tonight." He rubbed his ears. "They're still ringing. You have a mean punch. Where did you learn to take care of yourself?"

"A matter of survival in a tough neighborhood." That was true, but she'd also had additional training in the army.

"As my grandmother said, that isn't an issue here. We're on a side of a mountain miles away from the nearest town. No one bothers us up here."

If you only knew. "I'm licensed to carry—"

But Mrs. Winfield's grandson ignored her protest and descended the staircase.

Ellie rushed to the railing overlooking the downstairs entrance. Clutching the wood, she leaned over and said, "That's my weapon. I'll take care of it."

"That's okay. I'm taking care of it." Then he disappeared into the hallway that led to the office where the safe was.

"I certainly understand why you got scared." Mrs. Winfield approached her at the railing and patted her back. "I did when I heard the noise from you two in the hallway. I didn't know what was happening. I appreciate you being willing to protect me, but thank goodness, it wasn't necessary."

This time. Ellie swung around to face the older woman. "Yeah, but you never know."

"The Lord watches out for His children. I'm in the best care."

"I agree, but that doesn't mean we shouldn't be proactive, Mrs. Winfield," Ellie said, hoping to convince Mr. Jefferson to tell her about the threats tomorrow.

"Please call me Winnie. Christy, my previous assistant, did. I don't like standing on formality since you'll be helping me." She smiled. "Colt gave me that name years ago, and everyone calls me that now."

"Was he supposed to visit?"

"The last I heard he wasn't going to come back this year for Christmas. He probably heard my disappointment when we talked on the phone a few days ago. If I had known Colt was coming, I would have said something to you."

She'd read the dossier Kyra Hunt had given her on Colt Winfield, the only grandson Mrs. Winfield had. She should have recognized him, but with a beard and scruffy hair and disheveled clothes he'd looked like a bum who had wandered into the house intent on ill gains.

"He was supposed to be in the South Pacific on the research vessel through Christmas and the New Year." Mrs. Winfield gave Ellie a smile, her blue eyes sparkling. "Just like him to forget to tell me he was coming home after all for Christmas. Knowing him, it could be a surprise from the very beginning. He loves doing that kind of thing. Such a sweet grandson." She leaned close to Ellie to whisper the last because Colt Winfield was coming back up the steps.

"I wish that were the case, Winnie." Colt paused on the top stair. "But I need to get back to the *Kaleidoscope*. I managed to get a few days off before we start the next phase of our project, and I know how important it is to you that we have some time together at Christmas."

Great, he'll be leaving soon.

"Just a few days?" His grandmother's face fell, the shine in her eyes dimming. "I haven't seen you in months. Can't you take a couple of weeks out of your busy schedule to enjoy the holidays like we used to?"

Please don't, Ellie thought, rolling her shoulders to ease the ache from their tussle on the hardwood floor.

He came to the older woman and drew her into his embrace. "I wish I could. Maybe at the end of January. The government on the island is allowing a limited amount of time to explore the leeward side and the underwater caves."

Mrs. Winfield stepped away. "You aren't the only one on the research team. Let someone else do it for a while. You're one of three marine biologists. And the other two are married to each other. They get to spend Christmas together."

"I need to be there. Something is happening to the sea life in that part of the ocean. It's mutating over time. It's affected the seal population. You know how I feel about the environment and the oceans."

"Fine." Mrs. Winfield fluttered her hand in the air as she swept around and headed for the door to her bedroom. "I can't argue with you over something I taught you. Good night. I'll see you tomorrow morning. I hope you'll at least go for a power walk with Ellie and me. Seven o'clock sharp."

"Yes, Winnie. I've brought my running shoes. I figured you'd want me to."

When her employer shut the door to her room, Ellie immediately said, "I need my gun back."

"You do? What part of your duties as my grandmother's assistant requires you to have a gun?" His gaze skimmed down her length.

Ellie finally peered down at the clothes she wore—old sweats and a baggy T-shirt. With a glance at the mirror at the end of the hall, she noticed the wild disarray of her hair. She looked as scruffy as Colt Winfield. She certainly wouldn't appear to this man as a capable and efficient bodyguard. Or a woman who knew how to use a gun when she needed to. "Ask yourself. What if you had been a burglar? Would you have wanted me to let you rob the place or do worse?"

For half a moment he just stared at her, then he started chuckling. "Since I'm not and I'll be here for a few days, you'll be safe. Didn't you wonder why the three German shepherds didn't bark?"

"I know that dogs can be good for security purposes, but they can be taken out. It shouldn't be the only method a person uses." Which Mr. Jefferson was changing—just not fast enough for her liking. A new alarm system for the house would be in place by the end of the week. But even that didn't guarantee a person was totally safe. Hence the reason why Mr. Jefferson hired her to guard Mrs. Winfield—Winnie.

"So you decided to bring a gun."

"I'm very capable. I was in the army."

"Army? Even knowing that, I'm afraid, Miss St. James, we're not going to see eye to eye on this." He swiveled around and went to pick up a duffel bag by the steps. He hadn't had that when he'd first come upstairs. He must have brought it up when he put the gun in the safe. "Good night."

Ellie watched him stride down the corridor in the opposite direction of her bedroom. When he paused before a door at the far end, he slanted a look back at her. For a few seconds the corners of his mouth hitched up. He nodded his head once and then ducked inside.

She brought her hand up to comb her fingers through her hair and encountered a couple of tangles. "Ouch!"

Moving toward her bedroom, she kept her eye on his, half expecting him to pop back out with that gleam of humor dancing in his eyes. When he didn't, something akin to disappointment flowed through her until she shoved it away. She would have to call Mr. Jefferson to tell him that Colt was here. From what she'd read about the man he was smart, with a doctorate in marine biology as well as a degree in chemistry. Currently he worked on a research vessel as the head marine biologist for a think tank formed to preserve the world's oceans.

His grandmother hadn't ever questioned why Ellie was always around, even in her lab, but she had a feeling Colt would. Then he would demand an answer.

After traveling for almost twenty-four hours the day before, Colt dragged himself out of bed at a quarter to seven in his old room where he'd grown up. Winnie hadn't changed anything in here, and he doubted she ever would. She would always think of him as her little boy. Although Winnie was his grandmother, she'd raised him when his own mother had died from a massive infection shortly after he was born. Thinking of his past brought both heartache and joy. Heartache because he'd lost so many people he cared about. But he'd rather not dwell on his past. Besides, he had Winnie. She had given him so much.

After dressing in his sweats to power walk in the crisp December air in the Colorado mountains, he made his way toward the kitchen and the scent of coffee. Just its aroma made his body crave caffeine. He'd need it if he was going to keep up with Winnie. At seventy-three, she was an amazing woman, owner of Glamour Sensations and creator of both women's and men's fragrances. Not to mention her latest development—a line of antiaging products rumored to revolutionize the cosmetic industry. This had been a dream of Winnie and his granddad for fifteen years. Although his grandfather was dead, Winnie was close to completing their vision with the development of a cream that faded scars and lines as though they had never been there in the first place.

Clean-shaven, Colt came into the kitchen to find his grandmother and her new assistant sitting at the table drinking mugs of coffee. "I thought you would be gone for your power walk by now, leaving me with the whole pot of coffee."

His grandmother glanced at the clock on the wall. "As usual, ten minutes late. Did I not tell you we would have to wait on him, Ellie?"

The pretty assistant, dressed in a navy blue jogging suit with her long curly blond hair tamed into a ponytail, gave him a sugary sweet smile, a sparkle in her brown eyes. "I tried to talk her into leaving without you, but she insisted on waiting."

He made his way to his grandmother, kissed her cheek then headed for the pot to pour some coffee.

"You won't have time for that. I have a meeting with Harold at eight-thirty, and I'm sure he would want me to shower and change before we meet in the lab." Winnie rose and took a last swallow from her mug before setting it on the table. "You can have some later."

"What if I walk off the side of the mountain because I fell asleep?" He put his empty cup on the counter.

"Dear, if you manage to fall asleep while power walking with me, I'll be surprised. Besides, we're walking inside the fence. It would stop your fall."

"Your power walking is grueling." Taking up the rear, he followed the two women out onto the wooden deck along the back of the redwood and glass house that sat in a meadow with a high fence around the premises.

As though expecting Winnie at that time of the day, the three German shepherds sat near the door, their tails wagging. Rocket, the white one, barked his greeting.

His grandmother stooped over and patted each one, saying, "I've got a treat for you later today. A juicy bone. I know how much you like that."

Lady, the only female, nudged his grandmother's hand for more scratches behind the ear. Winnie laughed. "You always demand more attention than the boys here. They may be larger, but I have a feeling they do whatever you want."

Standing next to Ellie and watching the exchange between his grandmother and the guard dogs, Colt said, "My grandfather bought Rocket and Gabe to be company and guard the place seven years ago. He was very attached to them. Winnie went out and purchased Lady from the same trainer. She wanted female representation. They love staying outside, but whenever the weather gets bad, she brings them inside, even though they have a top-of-the-line dog structure."

"I've seen it. It isn't your ordinary doghouse. I thought it might be a storage shed until I saw them going in and out."

"That's because nothing is too good for her dogs. When Granddad died, Winnie took over all three dogs' care with her caretaker's help."

When she finished greeting each pet, Winnie went through some stretches. "Colt, I don't want to hear any complaining on my walk. You're in perfectly good shape."

"I don't complain. I tease."

"I have a feeling you swim every day you have a chance on the job. Ellie, he can swim ten miles without tiring. Not to mention he can hold his breath underwater for two minutes. I think that's from growing up here in the mountains. Great lung capacity."

His grandmother's remark to her assistant slid his attention to the tall woman who lunged to the left then right. "So you're into power walking, too?"

Ellie brought her feet together, raised one leg behind her and clasped her ankle. "When I can get the chance, I usually jog, but I've been enjoying our early morning jaunts."

"Who did you work for before this?"

Pausing, she stretched her other leg. "A small company," she said finally.

Winnie didn't seem to notice the slight hesitation in Ellie's reply, but he did. Was something going on? When he got back from his power walk, he would catch Harold before he talked with Winnie. He didn't want to upset his grandmother unless there was a good reason, but who exactly was Ellie St. James? A woman who carried a gun and, based on last night, wasn't afraid to use it.

"I'm glad I caught you before you talked with Winnie." Ellie shut the library door after the lawyer entered.

"Ah, I see you've made good progress with Winnie," Harold Jefferson said. "She doesn't usually have someone call her Winnie unless she likes you."

"I think that's because she appreciated my attempt to protect her last night."

His eyebrows shot up. "Someone got in the house? Why didn't you call me?"

"Because it turned out to be her grandson."

His forehead wrinkled. "Colt's here?"

"Yes, for a few days. I thought he was an intruder and I pulled my gun on him in the upstairs hallway. Without her knowing why I'm here, she doesn't understand why I would have a gun. It's now sitting in her safe in her office. That ties my hands protecting her. She needs to be told."

"She will stress and shut down. She's under a tight deadline with this new product she's coming up with. That's why I'm here to talk to her about the publicity campaign now that her former assistant, Christy, has agreed to be the new face for the company."

"The Winnie I've seen this past week is tough when she needs to be."

"It's all a show. I've been through a lot with her. Years ago her company nearly fell apart because of her son's death. Then she had a heart attack ten years ago, and we went through another rough patch. That was followed by her husband passing away five Christmases ago.

Finally she's close to going public with Glamour Sensations and offering stock as she brings out her new line, Endless Youth. She's been working toward this for years. She feels she needs to fulfill her late husband's vision for the business."

Ellie placed her hand on her waist, trying to control her frustration and impatience. "If she is dead, she won't be able to fulfill his vision."

"That's why you're here. To keep her alive. The fewer people who know someone has sent her threats the better. She *is* the company. The brains and creative force behind it. We need the infusion of money to make a successful campaign for the new products in the spring that will lead up to the unveiling of the signature cream next Christmas."

"If the company is going public, don't you have to disclose the threats?"

"Yes. When we reach that part of the process, we'll have to disclose the threats to the investment banker and lawyers. Fortunately, we have until right after Christmas to take care of the problem."

"I can't protect her without my weapon. It's that simple."

"What if we tell Colt and have him get the gun for you? She rarely goes into the safe. I imagine she's too busy in the lab downstairs."

Ellie looked out the floor-to-ceiling window across the back at the stand of pine trees. "Yes, but what if she does?"

She'd never liked the fact that Mrs. Winfield didn't know about the threats and the danger her life was in. The former assistant had given Mr. Jefferson each threatening letter. They had become more serious over the past month, and one also included a photo of Mrs. Winfield out power walking. That was when he had contacted Guardians, Inc. He was hoping nothing would come of the letters, but he knew he had to put some kind of protection in place. That was when Ellie had entered as the new assistant to replace Christy Boland, who was going to be the spokesperson for Glamour Sensations' Endless Youth line.

"On second thought, we probably shouldn't tell Colt. I don't want anyone else to know if possible. He might let something slip to his grandmother. It's probably better that he returns to the research ship." Mr. Jefferson snapped his fingers. "I've got it. I'll get you a gun to use. I can come back out here this afternoon with whatever you want. Maybe a smaller gun that you can keep concealed."

"Fine, unless I think there's a direct threat."

"I'm hoping I can catch the person behind the letters before then. The Bakersville police chief is working on the case personally, as well as a P.I. I hired. Winnie received another letter at headquarters yesterday."

"Another picture in it?"

"No, just threats of what the person is going to do to her."

Ellie thought of the sweet lady she'd spent the past week with—a woman who toiled long hours because she knew a lot of people who worked for her counted on her. "What in the world has she done to anger someone?"

"We're looking into disgruntled employees, but she was never directly responsible for firing anyone. If she had her way, everyone would still be working for her no matter if they didn't do their job. Thankfully I run that part of the business."

Ellie sighed. "I'll need you to bring me a Glock G27. It's smaller and easily concealed. It will have to do, even though I prefer my own weapon. At least you were able to get Winnie to stay and work from home this month. That will help the situation, but this home isn't secure."

"Is any place?"

"No, but there are some things we can do."

"Like what? I'm working on a better security system."

"That's good because the one she has is at least ten years old." Ellie paced the large room with bookcases full of books. "We could use bulletproof windows. Security guards to patrol the grounds and posted at the gate. Also cameras all over the house and the property being monitored 24/7."

"She won't go for anything else. She didn't even understand why I wanted to upgrade her security system. Told me the Lord was looking out for her and that's all she needs."

Ellie believed in the power of God, but Winnie was being naive. "What if someone gets to her? I've convinced her that I enjoy power walking, and she has graciously asked me to come with her, but she likes her independence. I'm running out of reasons to tag along with her when she leaves this house."

"It's only for a couple of more weeks at best. The P.I. on the case is tracking down some promising leads. If nothing changes after she has completed the last product for this new line, I'll tell her. She's fragile when she's in her creative mode. Easily distracted. Even Colt's visit will strain her schedule."

"And Christmas won't? I get the impression she enjoys the holiday." The wide-open space outside the window made her tense. Someone could be out there right now watching their every move.

"That's just a few days." Mr. Jefferson checked

his watch. "I'd better find Winnie. She starts to worry when people are late."

"I've noticed that."

"Five years ago next week, Thomas was on the way home from work and lost control of his car. It went off the cliff. The sheriff thought he'd fallen asleep at the wheel from reports by witnesses. So anytime someone is late she begins to think the worst." He covered the distance to the door. "I'll meet with Winnie in the lab then come back later with your gun."

"So let me get this straight. You don't want to tell Colt?" Another secret she would have to keep.

Looking back at her, Mr. Jefferson opened the door. "No, not right now."

"Not right now what?" Colt stepped into the entrance of the library.

Chapter Two

Mr. Jefferson waved his hand and passed Colt quickly in the hall. "I'll let Miss St. James tell you."

Ellie balled her hands at her sides. What was she supposed to tell Colt? Even worse, had he overheard anything they had been talking about? She started forward. "I'd better go and change for work."

He gripped her arm, halting her escape. "What aren't you telling me? Why were you and Harold talking in here?"

She schooled her expression into one of innocence. She would love to get her hands on Mr. Jefferson for putting her in this situation. "He wanted to know how my first week went with Winnie. Is there a reason we shouldn't talk? After all, he hired me."

"And how are you doing?" He stepped nearer

until Ellie got a whiff of his coffee-laced breath. "Does he know about the gun?"

"Yes. I saw no reason not to tell him." Her heartbeat kicked up a notch. She moved back a few inches until her back encountered the wall behind her. "Your grandmother and I are getting along well. She's a special lady. Very talented. She's easy to talk to. To work for."

"Winnie?"

Hating the trapped feeling, she sidled away. "Who else are we talking about?"

"My grandmother is a private woman. She doesn't share much with anyone."

"I haven't found her that way. Maybe something has changed, since you've been gone for so long." There, she hoped that would keep Colt quiet and less curious about her relationship with Winnie. In some of her past jobs, she'd had to play a role, but it never was her favorite way to operate.

"Then maybe you can fill me in on what's going on with my grandmother."

"What we've talked about is private. If you want to know, go ask her." Before he could stop her again, she pivoted away and hurried down the hall to the foyer.

As she mounted the stairs to the second floor, she felt his eyes on her. It was so cold it reminded her of the icy mountain stream they'd passed on their walk today. Unable to shake loose of his frosty blue gaze, she felt the chill down to her bones.

After dinner that evening Ellie followed the small group to the den, a room with a roaring fire going in the fireplace and the dark rich wood of the mantel polished to a gleaming luster that reflected the lights. She sat on the plush, tan couch before a large glass-topped coffee table. In the middle an arrangement of sweet-smelling roses vied with the fireplace for attention. She'd quickly learned Bloomfield Flower Shop in the medium-size town at the foot of the mountain delivered a fresh bouquet twice weekly because Winnie loved looking at them in the evening. Their delicate aroma wafted up to Ellie and surrounded her in their fragrance. Since working for Winnie, she'd become attuned to the smell of things. Like breakfast in the morning or a fresh winter day with pine heavy in the air when they were power walking. Winnie always pointed out scents wherever she went.

Colt took a forest-green wingback chair across from her. She caught his glance lingering on her for a few extra seconds while the others settled into their seats. She pulled her gaze away to finish assessing the placement of everyone, along with all the exits. Harold took the other end of the couch she sat on while Winnie eased down between them. Christy Boland, the face of the new line, and her fiancé, Peter Tyler, a Bakersville dentist, occupied the love seat.

"I can't imagine living on a research vessel for months on end," Christy said, taking up the conversation started at the dinner table.

"I have to admit it does take getting used to. It was an opportunity I couldn't pass up. I don't even have a place of my own right now."

"You don't need one. You're always welcome here when you're in the country," Winnie told her grandson. "After all, you've done so much to help me with my new line, especially this last product, which will be the coup d'état."

"How so, Winnie? I don't remember doing that."

"Your research on certain sea life sparked a breakthrough for me on this project."

Colt tilted his head to the side. "Which one?"

Winnie smiled. "I'm not telling. Right now I'm the only one who knows. It's all up here." She tapped the side of her temple. "But this will keep you busy for years, Christy. Harold isn't going to be able to count the money fast enough." Her grin grew. "At least that's what I predict. And all my predictions have been right in the past." She sat back and motioned the servers to bring in dessert.

Linda and Doug Miller, the middle-aged couple who lived on the property and took care of the house, carried in two trays, one with coffee and the other with finger sweets. Doug placed the coffee down in front of Winnie while his wife served the petite desserts to each person in the room.

"I will say I miss your cooking, Linda. No one on the vessel can cook like you." Colt selected four different sweets and put them on a small plate.

By the time the caretakers retreated to the kitchen ten minutes later, everyone had a cup of coffee and dessert.

Colt raised his cup in a toast. "To Christy. Congratulations again on becoming the face of Endless Youth. This is a big change for you from being Winnie's assistant to touring the country, your photo plastered everywhere."

"Yes. I haven't traveled like you have or Winnie. About as far as I've gone was Texas and California when Winnie did."

"That will definitely change, dear," Winnie said after taking a sip of her coffee. "I'm thrilled you agreed to do this. When you tested the product and it did such wonders for you, it became obvious you were perfect for this new job." She slid a glance toward Harold. "Thankfully, Harold found a new assistant for me who is working out great."

All eyes turned to Ellie. Never wanting to be the focus of attention, she pressed herself into the couch until she felt the Glock in its holster digging into her back. Harold had brought the gun when he'd returned for dinner. Having it holstered under her jacket was a constant reminder she was on a job. "I appreciate you helping me, Christy. Answering my hundreds of questions."

Christy laughed. "I wish I had someone to answer my hundreds of questions. I've never been a model and don't know one. Poor Peter has to listen to all my questions."

"And I don't have any answers for her. Actually, she's been gone so much lately that I haven't had to listen to them." Peter covered Christy's hand that lay between them on the love seat. "I'm looking forward to some togetherness at Christmas."

Harold bent forward to pour himself some more coffee. "I just finalized some plans for Christy to start the filming of the first commercial in L.A. next week."

Christy glanced at Peter then Harold. "But I'll be here for Christmas Day, won't I? It'll be our first Christmas together."

"Yes, but since we're launching part of the line in February for Valentine's Day, your time will be very limited."

Peter picked up her hand and moved it to his lap. "We'll work out something," he said to Christy, his adoring look roping her full attention.

As Ellie listened to the conversation shift to the launch of Endless Youth, she decided to call Kyra, her employer, and have her look into everyone around Winnie, including Harold Jefferson, who ran the day-to-day operation of Glamour Sensations as the CFO. She'd learned quickly not to take anything for granted, even the person who hired her.

The threats against Rachel Winfield had started when news of Endless Youth leaked to the press. What was it about that product line that would make someone angry with Winnie? From what Ellie had learned, the development and testing didn't upset any environmental groups. So did Endless Youth have anything to do with the threats or was its development and launch just a coincidence? Maybe it was a rival cosmetic company. Was the industry that cutthroat? Did this involve an industrial spy?

She kneaded her hand along her nape, trying to unravel the knots twisting tighter in her neck. Finding the person behind the threats wasn't her priority—keeping Winnie alive and unharmed was. She needed to leave the rest to the police and Harold's P.I.

* * *

Colt entered the kitchen that gleamed with clean counters, any evidence of a dinner party gone, but the scent of the roast that Linda had cooked still lingered in the room. The Millers did wonders behind the scenes for Winnie and had worked for the family for ten years. He wasn't sure what his grandmother would do if they decided to look for another job. He didn't worry about Winnie with Linda and Doug taking care of the property and house.

He raided the refrigerator to make himself a sandwich with the leftover roast beef. After piling it between slices of Linda's homemade bread, he turned away from the counter ready to take a bite. But he halted abruptly when he noticed Ellie hovering in the entrance, watching him.

She blinked and averted her gaze. "I heard a noise and came to check it out. Winnie just went to bed."

"She stayed up later than usual, but then when Christy and Harold come to dinner, she usually does. That's the extent of her entertaining here."

"I can see that. She spends most of her day in the lab."

"My grandmother is one of the few people in the world who has a 'nose,' as they say in the perfume industry. She can distinguish different scents and has a knack for putting them together to complement each other. That comes easy for her. But this new product line is something else, more Granddad's pet project. I'll be glad when she finishes and doesn't have to work so much."

Ellie came into the room. "She's being taken care of. Linda makes sure she eats healthy. Harold doesn't let her worry about the running of Glamour Sensations, and I do all the little things she has allowed to mount up."

"So she can focus on Endless Youth. I can remember when Granddad was alive. Those two talked about the line back then. He had already started the research. Winnie is just finishing up what they began in earnest eight years ago. I think he pushed her to help her recover from her heart attack. She loves a good challenge." He held up his plate. "I can fix you one."

Her chuckles floated through the air. "I think I'll pass on that. I ate more tonight than I usually do."

He put his sandwich on the kitchen table and gestured at a chair beside him. "Join me. I hate eating alone. When you live on a small ship with fifteen others, you're rarely alone except in your tiny cabin. You would think I would cherish this time."

"You don't?" Ellie slid into the seat next to him.

He noticed she didn't wear any fragrance

and wondered if Winnie would change that. "I'm used to it so it's strange when I'm not here. When I've come back here, I've felt the isolation I never felt while I was growing up here."

"Well, it won't feel isolated too much longer. Winnie has several evening events the closer we get to the holidays."

"Let me guess. Most of them have to do with the business."

"Yes, and she is the mistress of ceremony at the lighting of the Christmas tree in Bakersville in a few days. This year the town is naming the park after your grandparents."

"They've been trying to get her to light the Christmas tree for years. I'm glad she finally accepted."

A tiny frown made grooves between Ellie's eyebrows.

"You aren't?" Colt asked.

Her expression evened out. "I'm only concerned she doesn't wear herself out. She has the big gala for Endless Youth and Christy's introduction to the press a few days after that."

"Yeah, she's been trying to get me to stay an extra week."

"I can understand the demands of work."

"Is this job demanding to you? Is the isolation getting to you?"

"I love the isolation. Remember, I grew up in Chicago where everywhere I turned there were people."

"How did you find out about this job?"

Ellie rose. "I think I'll fix a cup of tea. Do you want any? Herbal, no caffeine." She walked to the cabinet where the tea was kept and withdrew a tin of lavender tea.

"No, thanks." He waited until she put the water on to boil then continued, "Harold said something about him finding you. How? Chicago is a far piece from here."

"Harold knew my former employer. She suggested me for the job."

"She let you go?"

"Not exactly. She knew how much I love the mountains and thought this would be perfect for me."

"What did you do at your former job?"

She laughed. "I feel I'm being interviewed again, but since I already have the job, that isn't it. So why the interest?"

"Because I love Winnie and have her best interest at heart."

Gripping the counter edge with both hands, Ellie lounged back, except that there was nothing casual about her stance. Something wasn't right. Colt lived in close quarters and had learned to read people accurately and quickly. It made his life much easier and calmer.

"What are you hiding, Ellie?"

busied herself pouring the hot
ingredients, all until at once the entire...
"Where you hiding him."

Chapter Three

"What makes you think I'm hiding something?" Ellie busied herself pouring the hot water into a mug and dunking the tea bag.

"I get the feeling there's something in your past you don't like to talk about. If it wasn't that Harold is thorough when it comes to my grandmother, I would be concerned at your evasiveness."

"But Harold is thorough." She drew herself up straight, cupping her hands around the mug. "I didn't know full disclosure about all the details of my life was necessary for me to get this job. Winnie seems satisfied. Is this something we should bring up to her?" Lifting her chin, she clamped her jaws together to keep from saying anything else that would get her fired.

He dipped his head in a curt nod. "Duly noted. Winnie is a great judge of character."

Meaning he had his doubts? Pain shot down her neck from the tense set of her teeth grinding together. She strode to the table and took the chair across from him. Though she would rather drink her tea in peace, she knew escaping to her bedroom would only confirm that she had something to hide.

One of the reasons she liked being a bodyguard was that she could blend into the background. Most of her clients didn't engage her in casual conversation. But Winnie had been different, and it seemed to run in the family. She kept a lock on her past—a past she didn't want to take out and reexamine. No point in going over it.

"If you must know, the short version of my life so far is—"

"That's okay—"

"I grew up in Chicago," she interrupted, "in a part of town where I had to learn to take care of myself and stick up for my brother, too. People weren't kind to him. He had a mental disability and talked 'funny.' Their word, not mine. When I could get out of the neighborhood, I did." She sipped her tea, gripping the mug tighter to keep her hands steady.

"Where's your brother?"

"Dead." The word hung in the air between them for a long moment while Ellie relived the moment when Toby had slipped away from congestive heart failure.

"I'm sorry. I didn't mean to bring up something painful."

"What did you mean to do, then?"

"To make sure Winnie was in good hands."

She stared into his light, gray-blue eyes. "She's in good hands. When I do a job, I do it one hundred percent."

Another long silence stretched between them as she felt the probe of his gaze, seeking, reading between the lines.

"Did I pass?" She raised her cup and drank, relishing the warm, soothing tea.

"This wasn't a test."

"You could have fooled me." After she scooted back her chair, the scraping sound filling the kitchen, she pushed to her feet. "While I would love to continue this interrogation—I mean conversation—I'm tired and plan to go to bed. Good night."

She left the kitchen. Out in the hallway she paused, a hand braced on the wall as images of her twin brother washed through her mind—running from the neighborhood bullies, falling and scraping his palms and shins, crying because he didn't understand why they didn't like him. But the worst picture was of Toby on the floor of their small, dirty apartment, taking his last breath. He looked straight at her. She held him while they waited for the ambulance. A light brightened his eyes, and a peace she'd never seen fell over his face. Then he went limp as the sirens came down the street. She'd been thirteen.

Tears crowded her eyes. She squeezed them closed. This was why she never dwelled in the past. She did not shed tears—hadn't since she was thirteen.

She slowly crossed to the front door and checked to make sure it was locked and the antiquated security system was on. After Colt went to bed, she would make a more thorough check of the house before she slept. Until then she would prowl her bedroom, hating the situation she'd been placed in. This secrecy handicapped her doing her job.

Standing in the dark, Colt stared out his bedroom window at the yard in front of the house; the outdoor lights illuminated the circular drive. Usually by this time of year there was a lot of snow on the ground, but not so far this winter. Most Christmases as a child, he remembered it being white. This year he'd be in the middle of the Pacific Ocean with blue water as far as he could see. One morning at the beginning of the week, a day after he'd talked to Winnie, a

strong urge had overcome him. He needed to
see his grandmother if only for a short time.
He couldn't shake the feeling all that day. By
nighttime he'd made a reservation to fly back
to Colorado.

He glanced at his bed. He needed to sleep.
Wanted to sleep. But he couldn't. Winnie's new
assistant plagued his thoughts. Something didn't
fit. First, although she and Winnie seemed to
get along great, Ellie wasn't his grandmother's
usual type of assistant. Christy had fit the mold
well for three years. Accommodating. Almost
meek. A follower, not a leader.

But Ellie certainly wasn't meek. He rubbed
his ear, recalling her defensive tactic last night.
And accommodating? Hardly. He had thought
for a minute that she was going to tackle him for
her gun. But mostly she wasn't a follower. Although she'd done everything his grandmother
had requested of her today, her mannerisms
and actions spoke of a woman in command. A
woman who wouldn't admit to a vulnerability.

A couple of hours ago, though, he'd seen a
crack in her defenses when she'd talked about
her childhood, her brother. That was what he
couldn't get out of his mind. The glimpse of
pain in her eyes he suspected she didn't realize she'd shown. Or maybe she did and couldn't
control it because the hurt went so deep.

Staring at the play of light and dark surrounding the front of the house, Colt plowed his fingers through his hair. His skin felt as if he was swimming through a swarm of jellyfish, their tentacles grazing across his arms and legs, their touch sending pain through him.

Something wasn't right. He couldn't shake that feeling, just as he couldn't deny the need to come see Winnie a few days ago.

One of the German shepherds that guarded the property pranced across the drive and disappeared into the dark. Squinting, Colt tried to follow the dog's trek. Something white flashed out of the corner of his eye, so briefly he wasn't sure he'd seen anything. He shoved away from the window and headed for the door. He wasn't sure why. It was probably nothing. One of the guard dogs had white fur.

Still. He wanted to check.

A sound in the foyer caught Ellie's attention. She'd just checked that part of the house. Was Winnie up? Colt? She crept down the hallway toward the front entrance, pulling her gun from the holster under her large sweatshirt. She found Colt crossing the foyer to the exit.

Relieved it was only him, she stuck the borrowed gun back into its holster and entered the entry hall. "Is something wrong?"

With his hand reaching for the doorknob, Colt jerked and pivoted toward her. "What are you doing down here? I thought you went to bed."

"And I thought you did, too."

"I did. Couldn't sleep."

"So you're going for a walk dressed like that? Won't you get cold?" She gestured at his sweatpants, T-shirt and bare feet.

He peered down. "I thought I saw something outside." Taking a few steps toward her, he took in her similar attire except for her bulky sweatshirt to cover her weapon and her tennis shoes, in case she had to give chase. "I'm sure it was nothing now that I think about it. Probably one of the dogs. If anyone had been outside, they would be barking."

Unless they were taken out, she thought, recalling her words to Colt earlier. "Dogs aren't invulnerable."

He paused. "True. I'd better check on it."

"I can. I'm dressed for it."

"Yeah, I noticed your tennis shoes."

She started toward the front door. "I don't have slippers, and I'm not accustomed to the cold."

"But you're from Chicago," Colt said as she passed him.

"We are seven thousand feet up the side of a mountain in December, and, besides, I've never been accustomed to the cold, even being from Chicago." Glancing at the alarm system, she noticed he'd turned it off. She grasped the handle and opened the door. As she stepped out onto the front deck, Colt followed her. "I've got this." *Leave it to a pro.* The urge to say those words was strong, but she bit them back.

"You're kidding. I'm not letting you come out here alone. What if someone is here? Who do you take me for?"

"Someone who only has pants and a T-shirt on and no shoes, not even socks. That's who." She ground her teeth together, wanting to draw her gun as she checked the area out. But he was probably right about it being one of the dogs.

"I'm used to the cold. I'm coming. End of discussion."

Patience. I could use a dose of it, Lord.

"Fine. Stay close behind me."

He chuckled in her ear. "Yeah, sure." Skirting around her, he descended the steps, quickly heading into the wisps of fog snaking along the ground.

Where's a stun gun when I need one? Ellie hurried after Colt who moved quickly from the cold concrete drive to the warmer lawn. "Wait up."

He didn't slow his pace, but she caught up with him about ten yards from the house. When she glanced back and spied the unprotected place, lit with security lights, she clamped her hand around his arm.

He halted, his face unreadable in the shadows.

"Go back and make sure no one goes into the house. I'll finish checking out here." Her fingers itched to draw her gun, but Mr. Jefferson didn't want Colt to know why she was here.

"And leave you alone? This is my home, not yours. What kind of man would I be?"

"A smart one. What about leaving your grandmother alone?"

"Then you should go back and—"

Barking blasted the chilled air.

Ellie withdrew the Glock from its holster and started toward the sound to the left.

"Where did that come from?" Colt asked.

"Mr. Jefferson."

"Harold?"

"I'll explain later. Go back to the house, lock the door and don't let anyone in until I check out what caused the dog to bark. Do not follow me."

"Who are you?"

No more secrets—at least with Winnie's grandson. "A bodyguard hired to protect Winnie." She glanced over her shoulder to make sure no one was trying to get into the front of the house. "Go. Now."

In the cover of night that surrounded them, he stared at her, or at least she felt the drill of his gaze, then he whirled around and rushed back toward the deck. She moved toward where the sound had come from, retrieving her small pocket flashlight in case she needed it. Right now she let the half-moon and security lamps by the house light her path since it would be better if she didn't announce her approach if someone was inside the fence.

In the distance she heard the cry of a mountain lion. She'd seen evidence of a big cat on one of her daily power walks with Winnie. Was that what spooked the dog? She'd gone into enough situations with incomplete intel to know the heightened danger that could cause.

Her heart rate kicked up a notch as she drew closer to the perimeter on the west side of the house where the eight-foot chain-link fence was. Another roar split the air. Closer. The sound pumped more adrenaline through her body. Every nerve alert, she became hyperaware of her surroundings—a bird flying away to the right, the breeze rustling the evergreen foliage.

Away from the house the only illumination was the faint rays of the moon. Not enough. She switched on her flashlight and swept it across the area before her. Just outside a cut part of the fence, its glow fell upon the mountain lion, its big eyes glittering yellow in the dark. Her light captured the predator's menacing stance.

The rumble of a mountain lion nearby froze Colt as he mounted the last step to the front deck. He knew that sound from the many years he had lived here. He didn't know who Ellie St. James really was, how capable she was or why she would be protecting his grandmother, but he couldn't leave her out there to face a solitary predator by herself. No matter what she ordered him to do.

He rushed into the house to a storage closet where Winnie kept some of his possessions. He used to have a hunting rifle. Wrenching the door open, he clicked on the overhead light and stared at the mountain of boxes that he had stored there. He delved into the midst of the containers filled with his memories. Where was the gun?

Panic urged him deeper into the large, walk-in closet to the shelving in the back. There he saw something he could use. Not the rifle but a speargun, a weapon he was even more familiar with and actually quite good at using.

He snatched it up and raced toward the foyer, grabbing a flashlight on the way. Before leaving, he set the alarm, then locked the front door behind him. Another growl announced to anyone around that this was the big cat's territory and not to trespass.

As Colt ran toward the west side of the property, he hoped there weren't any trees the mountain lion could climb that allowed him access to the area inside the fence. Usually the eight-foot barrier kept dangerous animals out, but it had certainly sounded like it was close to the house, possibly inside the fence.

Then a yell pierced the night. "Get back. Get away."

Those words from Ellie prodded him even faster.

Ellie never took her eyes off the mountain lion. It was still on the other side of the fence with his head sticking through the part that had been cut and peeled back to allow something big—like a man—through the opening. She waved her arms around. She didn't want to shoot the animal because it was a beautiful creature. But she would if she had to.

Its snarls protested her order to leave.

Still it didn't move back. Its golden gaze seemed to assess its chances of leaping the four or five yards' distance between them.

Bracing herself, Ellie lifted her gun and shone her flashlight into its eyes. It continued to stare at her.

Behind her she heard something rushing toward her. Another mountain lion? But they were solitary animals that guarded their territory. One of the dogs? The one that had barked earlier? Where were the other two?

She was calculating her chances with the mountain lion, then the new threat, when she heard a war cry, a bloodcurdling sound. The mountain lion shifted its golden regard to her right for a few seconds, then stepped back out of the hole and sauntered away as though out for an evening stroll. Some of the tension siphoned from her.

She threw a glance over her shoulder and saw a light in the dark moving her way. Colt. An intruder wouldn't announce his presence with a flashlight or a war cry.

She spun around and started for him. "What are you doing? You were supposed to stay at the house." Her light found him in the night, carrying a speargun. "*This time* you need to stay here and guard this hole. I need to make sure Winnie is okay."

When she passed him, he clasped her arm and halted her progress. "Hold it. Winnie is fine. I set the alarm and locked the door. What's going on?"

She stared at his hand until he dropped his arm to his side. "Did you check on her?"

"Well, no. But we never went far from the house."

"I'm going to check on her, then I'll be back. Will you stay here and make sure the mountain lion doesn't come back? And this time stay where you're supposed to be. I could have shot you." She peered at his speargun. "A bit odd to be carrying around on dry land, but it should stop the cat if it returns. That is, if you can use it."

He pulled himself up straight. "I'm quite good with this. And it's very effective if you know what you're doing. Which I do." Each word was spoken with steely confidence.

"Good." She hurried away, at the moment her concern for Winnie's safety paramount.

What if this was all a diversion? What if someone got into the house when they weren't looking? Different scenarios bombarded her. All she knew was she had to lay eyes on Winnie to be reassured she was all right.

She unlocked the front door and immediately headed for the alarm to put in the code. Then she took the stairs two at a time. When she saw Winnie's door open, she finally breathed.

A strong scent of urine—probably the big cat's—pervaded the air as Colt neared the gap in the fence. He stuffed the flashlight through a chain-link hole, and its glow shone into the wooded area outside of Winnie's property. After leaning the speargun against the fence within his quick reach, he pulled the snipped sides back into place, enough that he hoped would discourage the mountain lion from plowing its way inside.

Then he examined the ground.

Footprints were barely visible on the dry ground, but about five or six feet away, tire impressions in the dead weeds and grass were clearer. Someone had pulled a vehicle up to the fence.

He swung around and swept his flashlight around his grandmother's property and then it hit him: Where were the dogs? Why weren't they over here?

Ellie entered Winnie's bedroom, her gun drawn but at her side in case the older woman was in the room unaware of what was transpiring outside. She didn't want to frighten her with a gun being waved in the air—not two nights in a row. Halting a few feet inside, Ellie stared at the messy covers spilling over onto the floor, the empty bed. As she raised her weapon, she circled the room, checking for her client.

After opening the bathroom door, she noted the spacious area was empty.

As much as she would like to rush back outside and search the grounds for Winnie or any clue to her whereabouts, she had to check the house first.

As she started with the room next to Winnie's, prayers for the woman's safety flooded her thoughts. When she reached Colt's bedroom, she hesitated, feeling awkward to intrude on his privacy. But she had a job to do. She pushed open the door and looked inside.

This is ridiculous. If the man had followed her orders, she wouldn't have to do this right now. She stepped inside and made a quick tour—noting his duffel bag on a chair, his shoes on the floor, keys and some change on the dresser, pictures on the wall from when he was young.

A picture of him coming out of the darkness with a speargun in his hand crowded into her thoughts. She shook the image from her mind and turned to leave.

"What are you doing in my grandson's room with a gun in your hand?"

Chapter Four

"I was looking for you," Ellie said, putting the gun out of sight of Winnie in the doorway. "Someone has cut the fence and the guard dogs can't be found. I wanted to make sure you were all right." After picking up Colt's tennis shoes off the floor, she moved toward the exit.

"Where's my grandson? What are you doing with those shoes?" Winnie blocked her path.

"I'll explain everything after I call the sheriff and make sure Colt is okay. He's guarding the hole, making sure the mountain lion doesn't return. He's barefoot."

"The sheriff? A mountain lion? Colt barefoot in this weather? What in the world is going on?" What wrinkles Winnie had on her face deepened as she stepped to the side to allow Ellie to leave the room.

Ellie hurried toward the stairs, fishing for her

cell in her pocket. At the top she paused and glanced at the older woman. "I'm going to set the alarm. Please stay inside."

Winnie opened her mouth but snapped it closed before saying anything.

Ellie rushed down the stairs while placing a call to the sheriff's office outside Bakersville. After reporting what happened, she hit the buttons on the keypad to set the alarm and hastened outside.

The crisp night air burrowed through the sweatshirt, chilling her. The thought of Colt without shoes spurred her faster toward the fence line. When she arrived, he stood by the hole he'd partially closed, holding his spear gun while hugging his arms against his chest.

"I thought you could use these." She thrust his shoes at him, then shined her flashlight on the area beyond the fence.

"Thanks. I will never again leave the house in winter without my shoes on."

"Why did you?" She examined the set of tire tracks and boot prints, wishing it wasn't so dark.

"To protect you."

"Someone needs to protect you from yourself."

"You can't deny I helped you. Someone needed to guard this hole. Since you're back out here, I'm assuming Winnie is all right."

"Yes, and I called the sheriff's office." Ellie backed away, realizing there was nothing she could do until morning other than talk with the deputy who was on the way up the mountain. She had half a mind to call Harold Jefferson and wake him up with the news, but she would wait and give him a full report first thing in the morning. "Do you think there's anything at the house I can use to finish closing the bottom of this hole?"

"How about rope?" Colt started for his childhood home.

"That'll do." Ellie followed him. "I'm sure the mountain lion is long gone with all this activity, but I'll feel better when we have the hole completely closed."

"You don't think the person who cut the fence is inside here?"

"Probably not. Maybe the mountain lion scared him off or maybe his intent was to take the guard dogs. He could have tranquilized them. The ground looked like something was dragged toward the car."

"Why hurt the dogs?"

"It would take a while to get trained guard dogs to replace them. Maybe it was to scare Winnie like the threatening letters. When I find him, I'll ask him."

"When *you* find him? And what threatening letters?"

She reminded herself going after the person who was trying to harm Winnie wasn't her job. "I mean when the police find him, they'll ask him."

Colt unlocked the front door and hurried to the keypad to turn off the security system. Winnie sat on the third step on the staircase, her face tensed into a frown. She didn't move when both Colt and Ellie turned toward her.

"I need to check the house then I'll explain what's going on." She peered at Colt. "Would you stay here with your grandmother?"

He held up the speargun. "Yes. But the security system was on the whole time."

"This one can be circumvented quite easily if you know what you're doing. We have to assume whoever is after Winnie knows what he's doing," Ellie said in a low voice.

Winnie pushed to her feet. "Someone's after me? Who?"

Colt took a step toward his grandmother, glancing at Ellie. "I'll take care of her. Do what you need to do."

"What is going on, young man?" Winnie asked as Ellie hastened her exit.

As she went from room to room, she heard Colt trying to explain when he really didn't know much other than what she had told him. From her responses, Winnie was clearly not happy. Ellie decided not to wait until morning to call Harold.

"What's wrong?" the chief financial officer of Glamour Sensations asked the second he answered his phone.

After she explained what happened with the dogs and the fence, she said, "Not only does Colt know, but so does Winnie. I've called the sheriff's office, and one of the deputies is on his way."

"I'm calling Sheriff Quinn. Knowing him, he'll come, too. He lives halfway between Winnie's and Bakersville. It won't take him long to get there. I'll be there as fast as I can."

"You don't need to until tomorrow morning. After the sheriff leaves, I hope to get Winnie to go back to bed." She didn't want a three-ring circus at the house with so many people coming and going. That could be hard to secure.

"She won't do that. Maybe I should call her doctor, too."

"She seems okay." Ellie looked through the dining room into the living room where Colt had taken his grandmother. "She's sitting on the couch, listening to Colt."

"Fine. I won't call the doctor, but I'll be there soon."

Ellie pocketed her cell and made her way to the pair in the living room. "The house is clear."

Winnie shifted on the couch until her glare zeroed in on Ellie. "Who are you?"

"I told her you're here to protect her. That Harold hired you. But I don't know much more than that." Colt finally sat in the chair across from his grandmother.

With a sigh, Ellie sank onto the couch at the other end from Winnie. "I work for Guardians, Inc. It's a security company out of Dallas, staffed with female bodyguards. Mr. Jefferson came to my employer about his concerns that someone was threatening you. You have been receiving notes for the past six weeks, each one more threatening. He finally knew he had to do something when one included a photo of you on your power walk, dressed in what he discovered you'd worn the day before."

"Why didn't he come to me?" Winnie's mouth pinched into a frown.

"He's on his way, and he can answer that. I believe he thought it might interrupt your creative process and since the deadline is looming, he—"

"So that man kept it from me." Winnie surged to her feet. "I am not fragile like everyone thinks. Goodness me, I've been through enough and survived. That ought to give you all a hint at how tough I can be." She pivoted toward Ellie. "Is that why he neglected to tell me my new assistant was really a bodyguard?"

Ellie nodded. "I prefer full disclosure, but he was afraid of how—"

Winnie waved her quiet. "I know. I will take care of Harold. He promised my husband he would watch out for me, and he's taking his job way too seriously."

"Winnie, I don't know that he is." Colt leaned forward, clasping his hands and resting his elbows on his thighs. "Someone did cut the fence and the dogs are missing. Not one of them came up to us while we were outside. They always do."

Winnie blanched and eased down onto the couch. "So you really think there's a threat?" She looked from Colt to Ellie.

"Yes, especially after tonight." Ellie rose at the sound of the doorbell. "I'll get it."

She let the deputy and sheriff into the house. "I'm Ellie St. James. I was hired by Harold Jefferson to protect Mrs. Winfield."

Sheriff Quinn shook her hand. "Harold called me and told me. I understand the Bakersville police chief is looking into the matter of the threatening letters."

"Yes. I believe the person has upped his game. I haven't had a chance to search the whole property outside, but I feel the dogs have been taken. I did search the house and it's secured."

The sheriff turned to his deputy and said, "Take a look outside. Miss St. James, which part of the fence was cut?"

"The west side about halfway down."

"Let me know, Rod, when you're through checking the premises and the doghouse." Then to her, the sheriff asked, "Where's Winnie?"

"In the living room."

When the sheriff entered, Winnie smiled. "I'm so glad you're here, Bill. Did Ellie tell you what went on tonight?"

"Harold filled me in. It's a good thing Miss St. James and your grandson were here." The sheriff nodded toward Colt. "You couldn't have picked a better time to be home."

Winnie blew out an exasperated breath. "It would have been even better if they had clued me in on what was going on. Goodness, Bill, I've been out power walking. The man took a picture of me while I was."

"Maybe with all that has happened you should curtail that for the time being. It's gonna snow this weekend if the weather reports are correct." Sheriff Quinn sat on the couch where Ellie had been.

She assessed the law enforcement officer. He was probably in his early fifties but looked to be in excellent physical condition, well proportioned for his medium height with none of the potbelly she'd seen on others as they grew older and less active. She'd worked with her share of good ones and bad ones. From all of Harold's accounts, the sheriff fit into the good category. She hoped so because tonight the person after Winnie had stepped up his game.

She filled him in on what she'd seen outside. "Someone pulled a vehicle up to the fence recently. It rained hard a couple of days ago. The tracks could have been left maybe up to a day before, but they aren't deep enough for any longer than that. But I'm pretty sure it was this evening. We walk the perimeter every morning, and I haven't seen any evidence on the other side of the fence like what is there now. Also there are drag marks and a few paw prints beside those left by the mountain lion."

"So you think the tracks were made this evening?"

"Yes, Sheriff. That's the way it looks, but in the light of day we—you—might find more."

He smiled. "I'll take a look now. I've got a high-powered flashlight. I'll see where the tire tracks lead. The west side of the fence isn't the closest to the road out front."

"But it's the most isolated," Colt interjected.

Sheriff Quinn headed for the foyer. "When

he gets back I'm gonna leave Rod here. I'd like you to come with me, Miss St. James."

"Would you mind, Winnie?" Ellie asked her client, eager to go with the sheriff.

"No, go. I'll be well protected with Colt and the deputy."

As Ellie left, Colt told Winnie that he'd escort her to her bedroom. Ellie chuckled when the woman said, "Not on your life. I want to know what they find out there."

The doorbell sounded again while Ellie crossed the foyer. She'd relocked the door after the deputy had left. When she answered it, Harold stood there with the young officer.

He charged inside, slowing down only long enough to ask, "Where is she?"

"In the living room."

While he went to Winnie, the deputy came into the house. "I couldn't find any signs of the dogs. They're gone, Sheriff."

Quinn grumbled, his frown deepening. "Rod, stay with Mrs. Winfield." To Ellie, he said, "I don't like this. They were excellent, well-trained guard dogs."

"Yeah, that was the only part of the security here I liked." Ellie went ahead of the man onto the front deck.

"And possibly the only threat the person behind the letters needed to get rid of."

"Maybe. Something doesn't feel right."

"Any thoughts on what?"

"No. Just a vague feeling we're missing something." Ellie slipped into the sheriff's car.

As he drove to the road then toward the west part of the property, he said, "Harold told me the Bakersville police chief is looking into past employees. I can't believe one of them would be this angry with Winnie. She's the reason Bakersville is so prosperous. People around here love her."

"Someone doesn't. Maybe they aren't from around here. Maybe it's something we haven't thought about yet. Harold is having a private investigator look into Glamour Sensations' competition."

"Corporate sabotage?"

"It's a possibility. Winnie is the creative force behind the new line. From what I hear Endless Youth will change the playing field. It's not unheard of that a competitor will try to stop a product launch or beat a company to unveiling their own similar product."

"Mr. Winfield was the guy who talked me into running for sheriff twenty years ago. The best move I ever made. I owe the Winfield family a lot." He eased off the road and parked on the shoulder, directing a spotlight from his car toward the area where someone had driven off the highway and over the terrain toward the back of Winnie's property. "We'll go on foot from here."

Following the tire tracks led to the hole in the fence. Ellie knelt near the place where she'd seen the mountain lion's prints as well as smaller dog prints. No sign of blood or a struggle. When she had shined the light on the big cat earlier, she hadn't seen any evidence it had killed a dog. And she hadn't heard any noise to suggest that. So it meant the dogs had been taken recently by whoever drove the vehicle.

"These tire tracks look like they're from a truck or SUV. I'll have a cast made of them and see if we can narrow down the vehicle." The sheriff swung his high-powered light on the surrounding terrain. "These boot prints might help, too."

"It looks like about a size nine in men's shoes."

"Small man."

"Or a woman with large feet."

Ellie rose and searched the trees and brush. With some of the foliage gone because it was winter, she had a decent view. "No sign the dogs went that way."

"It doesn't look like it, but in the light of day we'll have better visibility and may find something. At the moment, though, I think the dogs were stolen. They're valuable. Maybe someone has kidnapped them."

"I don't think so. This is tied to the threats against Winnie somehow." Ellie ran her flashlight along the ground by the fence and caught sight of something neon green. She stooped and investigated closer. "Sheriff, I found something partially under this limb. I think it's from a dart gun. It would explain how he subdued the dogs so quickly."

The sheriff withdrew a small paper bag and gloves, then carefully picked up the long black dart with a sharp tip and a neon green cap on the opposite end. "Yup. I'll send this to the lab and see if there are any fingerprints on it. Hopefully they can tell us what was in the dart—poison or a knockout drug."

"At least there are a few pieces of evidence that might give you a lead."

As they walked back to the sheriff's car, Ellie kept sweeping her flashlight over the ground while Quinn scoured the terrain.

When he climbed into his patrol car, he said, "I have a friend who can repair the chain-link fence. I'll have him out here first thing in the morning. You don't want the return of the mountain lion."

"I'll be talking to Winnie and Harold about electrifying the fence and setting up a system to monitor the perimeter. If it hadn't been for the dogs, we might not have known about the hole in the fence for a while. That area is hidden by thick foliage from the house. We might not have seen it on our power walk in the morning, either."

"Yeah, she's definitely gonna have to beef up her security. She's been fortunate not to have problems in the past." As the sheriff returned to park in front of the main house, lights blazed from it. He chuckled. "She must have gone through and turned a light on in every downstairs room."

"I can't blame her. She all of a sudden realizes someone is after her."

Colt watched his grandmother as Harold explained his reasons for not letting her know what was going on with the letters. After he saw to Winnie, he was going to have a few words with Ellie and Harold. He should have been contacted right away when his grandmother first was threatened.

"The bottom line, Winnie, is that I didn't want you to worry about it when you have enough to deal with," Harold said.

Colt nearly laughed and pressed his lips together to keep from doing that. Harold was pulling out all the stops to persuade his grandmother not to be angry with him.

Her back stiff as a snowboard, Winnie narrowed her gaze on Harold, her hands clasped so tightly in her lap the tips of her fingers reddened. "I'm not a child, and you'd better remember that from now on, or no matter how long we have worked together, you'll be fired."

Harold swallowed hard. "My intentions were to protect you without worrying you. I have the police chief in Bakersville and a private investigator working on finding the person behind the letters."

"So you would never have told me if this hadn't happened. Was that your plan?"

Harold dropped his gaze to a spot on the carpet at his feet. Finally he nodded.

"I have to be able to trust you to inform me of *everything* that goes on at Glamour Sensations. Now I don't know if I can. What else are you keeping from me?" She lifted her chin and glared at her longtime friend.

Harold held up his hands, palms outward. "Nothing. But, Winnie, I promised Thomas I would look after you."

"I can look after myself. I have been for seventy-three years." Her rigid shoulders sagged a little.

Colt rose. "Winnie, let me escort you upstairs. We can hash this all out tomorrow."

She turned her glare on him. "Don't you start, young man. I don't need to be mollycoddled by you, too. I'll go to bed when I want to."

Harold interjected, "But you're starting the final tests tomorrow and—"

She swiveled her attention to him. "Losing a little sleep won't stop me from doing that. I'm not the fragile person you think I am. I want to hear what Sheriff Quinn has to say about the situation before I retire for the night. Or I wouldn't sleep a wink."

Colt heard the deputy greeting someone in the foyer. "I think they've returned."

Not five seconds later Ellie and Quinn came into the living room. Colt couldn't read much into Ellie's bland expression, but the sheriff's indicated there were problems, which didn't surprise him given what had happened an hour ago.

Sheriff Quinn stood at the end of the coffee table and directed his attention to Winnie. "Your guard dogs were drugged and stolen. We found a dart they used and tire tracks where they came off the main road, probably in a good-size four-wheel drive. Can't tell if it was a truck or SUV yet. A cast of the tire tracks might narrow it down for us."

Colt's gaze latched onto Ellie. She focused

on Winnie, too, except for a few seconds when she slid her attention to him. But her unreadable expression hadn't changed. He saw her military training in her bearing and the way she conducted herself. Ellie had certainly performed capably tonight, but what if the person after Winnie upped his tactics to more lethal ones?

When the sheriff finished his report, Winnie shook his hand. "Thank you, Sheriff Quinn. As usual you have done a thorough job. I want to be informed of any progress." She shifted toward Harold. "I want the Bakersville police chief and the private investigator you hired to be told that, too. No more secrets. Understood?" Her sizzling stare bore into the man.

Harold squirmed on the couch but locked stares with Winnie. "Yes, on one condition."

"You aren't in a place to dictate conditions to me. For several weeks you have kept me in the dark about something that concerned me. Don't push me, Harold Jefferson."

The color leaked from Harold's face. "I won't," he bit out, his teeth snapping closed on the last word.

"Good, I'm glad we understand each other now. That goes for you, too, Ellie and Colt. Also, I don't want this common knowledge, and I certainly don't want anyone to know that Ellie is a bodyguard. She is my assistant."

"Agreed," Harold said quickly. "Sheriff, can you keep this quiet?"

"Yes. All my deputies need to know is that someone took your dogs. Nothing about the reason or who you are, Miss St. James. We'll play this down."

"I appreciate that. I don't want a media circus until I'm ready to unveil my new line, and then I want the focus on Endless Youth, not me."

The sheriff nodded toward Winnie. "We'll be leaving. I'm going to post Rod outside your house."

"You don't have to do that. I have the very capable Miss St. James." Winnie winked at Ellie.

"Humor me, ma'am, at least for tonight."

"Fine."

Colt hid his smile by lowering his head. His grandmother would have her way in the end. The deputy would be gone by the morning, but Colt planned to have some other security measures in place by tomorrow evening.

Harold stood. "I'll show you out, Sheriff, and give you the name of my P.I. working on the case."

"I'm sorry that Harold put you in the position he did. He told me you wanted to inform me from the first. We'll proceed as usual, but my grandson will return your gun. I don't like weapons, so I'll ask you to keep it out of view." His grandmother struggled to her feet.

Colt rose quickly but didn't move toward Winnie. She would rebuke his offer to help, especially when he had made it obvious that he considered her fragile. In her mind she equated that to weak. His grandmother was anything but that. After all these years, Harold really didn't understand Winnie like Colt's grandfather had. If Harold had come to him, he would have told him his grandmother could handle anything.

He started toward the door when Winnie did.

She peered back at him. "Don't you buy into Harold's thinking I'm fragile. I hate that word. I am not going to break. Endless Youth was Thomas's project. I will complete it. I can find my own way to my bedroom. I have been doing that for years now."

Colt stopped and looked toward Ellie. Her mouth formed a thin line, but her eyes danced with merriment.

When Winnie left the room, Ellie took a seat on the couch. "I think she told you."

"It wasn't as bad as Harold got. He mismanaged this situation. All because he's in love with Winnie and doesn't really know her like he should."

"That's sad."

"I have a feeling my grandfather knew Harold

has been in love with Winnie since the early days. That's why he asked Harold to watch out for her. He knew he would. But Harold envisions himself as her knight in shining armor coming to her rescue. My grandmother is not a damsel in distress."

"What happened when your grandfather died?"

"She did fall apart. She'd nursed him back to health after his bout with cancer and was planning a month long vacation with him when he fell asleep behind the wheel and went off the mountain. For a short time, I saw her faith shattered. I was worried, but Harold was frantic and beside himself. He went into protective mode and hasn't let up since then."

Hearing footsteps nearing the doorway, Colt put his finger to his lips.

Harold came through the entrance, kneading his neck. "Winnie didn't even say good-night when she went upstairs. She really is mad at me."

"I'm afraid so." Colt waved his hand at the bouquet of flowers on the coffee table. "She isn't delicate like these roses. As soon as you accept that, you might have a chance with Winnie."

"A chance?" Harold opened his mouth to say more but clamped it shut.

Colt grinned. "Just so you know it, you have

my blessing to court my grandmother. I've known for a long time how you felt about her, and once this line is out, she deserves something more than working all the time. She's been driving herself for the past few years."

"What makes you think…" Harold's fingers delved into his neat hairstyle, totally messing it up.

"Because I see how you look at her when she isn't looking."

Harold's face flushed a deep shade of red. "She thinks I'm too young for her."

"You're sixty-five. That's not too young." Colt settled into his chair again. "Sit. We need to talk about securing the house and grounds."

"You stole my line," Ellie said as she angled toward Harold at the other end of the couch. "You need to electrify the fence, put in a new security system *tomorrow* and, since she doesn't want people to know what is going on, at least replace the guard dogs. That may be the biggest challenge. They need to be here with a handler right away."

Colt spoke up. "I have a high school friend who trains dogs. I'll give Adam a call tomorrow. If he has a dog for us, he only lives in Denver so he should be able to help us right away." He leaned back, trying to relax his body after the tense-filled past hour.

"This place needs a minimum of two dogs. Three would be better." Ellie looked at Harold. "How about the security system? The one in place is old and can be circumvented."

"I'll have someone here tomorrow. With the right kind of monetary incentive, I'm sure they could start right away. Maybe tomorrow afternoon. They probably could take care of the fence, too." Harold glanced toward the entrance into the living room. "Do you think Winnie will forgive my judgment call on this?"

"Her faith is strong, and she believes in forgiveness. I wouldn't be surprised if she isn't fretting right now about who she has angered enough to do this to her. Knowing her, she'll be praying for that person, whereas I would like to get hold of him and…" Colt let his words fade into silence, curling and uncurling his fists.

They didn't need to know he struggled with forgiving someone who had wronged him. He still couldn't forgive his father for all but abandoning him and going his merry way, living it up as if he didn't have a son and responsibilities. Winnie forgave his dad a long time ago, but after his mother had died, Colt had needed his only parent, and he hadn't been there for him.

"Well," Harold said, slapping his hand on the arm of the couch and pushing up, "I'd better be going. We all have a lot to do tomorrow."

"I'll walk you to the door and lock up after you leave," Ellie said, trailing after him.

Quiet settled around Colt like a blanket of snow over the landscape. Resting his head on the back cushion, he relished the silence, realizing this was what he needed after months on a small ship with cramped quarters. As thoughts of his job weaved through his mind, he knew he had to make a decision. Stay until Winnie was safe or leave and let others protect his grandmother. There wasn't really a decision, not where Winnie was concerned.

A movement out of the corner of his eye seized his attention. Ellie paused in the entrance, leaning her shoulder against the doorjamb. "Have you warmed up yet?"

"Finally I've thawed out. I may be used to living here in the winter, but remind me never to go outside in winter without shoes."

"You seemed lost in thought. I want to assure you I will do everything to protect Winnie. In the short time I've gotten to know her, I see what a special lady she is." She crossed the room and took her seat again across from him.

"We probably should follow Harold's example and get some rest, but I'm so wired right now with all that's happened."

"I know what you mean. Your adrenaline

shoots up and it takes a while to come down. But when it does, you'll fall into bed."

"I imagine with your job you've had quite a lot of experience with that. I can't say I have."

"One of the fringe benefits of being a bodyguard."

He laughed. "Never looked at it like that. How long have you been a bodyguard?"

"Three years. I started after I left the army."

"What did you do in the military?"

"For the last few years of my service I was in army intelligence."

"So that's where you learned your skills."

"Yes, it comes naturally to me now. Sometimes I only had myself to rely on when I was working alone in an isolated situation."

"Which I'm sure is classified top secret."

Her brown eyes lit with a gleam. "You know the cliché. If I told you, I'd have to kill you."

"I'm curious but not that curious. What made you go from army intelligence to being a bodyguard?" She intrigued him. It wasn't every day he met a woman who protected people for a living.

She shrugged. "It was my time to re-up, and I thought I would try something different. I had a friend who put me in touch with my employer. When I met Kyra, I knew this was what I wanted to do. I like protecting people who need it. I like the challenge in security."

"Why not police work?"

"I like to go different places. Kinda like you. I have a feeling you've seen a lot of the world through your work."

"Yes, and I've enjoyed it, but I've been on a ship a large part of that time."

"Tired of life on a boat?"

Am I? He hadn't stopped long enough to think about it. "The past few years have been hectic but fulfilling. I've learned a lot about sea life aboard the *Kaleidoscope.* But if Winnie had her way, she'd want me to use my knowledge for Glamour Sensations. She tells me I've inherited her nose."

Ellie studied that part of his face and frowned. "I think you look more like your grandfather." She gestured toward the portrait over the mantel.

"But I have her supersensitive smelling ability," he said with a chuckle. "Every time I come home, I get the spiel about taking over the family business. But if she goes public, it won't be a family business anymore."

"How do you feel about that?"

"I don't know. It's good for the company, but it means we'll be in the big leagues and I don't know how Winnie will really like that. This is

Harold's plan, and I understand why he is pushing to go public. The Endless Youth line will take us in a different direction. The expansion of the company will be good for this area."

Ellie tilted her head and smiled. "Do you realize you keep saying 'us' as though you are part of the company?"

"You'd make a good detective. Did you get your interview skills in the army?"

"I owe the army a lot, but I think I've always been nosy. It got me into trouble from time to time when I was growing up."

Colt yawned, the earlier adrenaline rush completely gone. "I guess that's my cue to get some sleep. Jet lag has definitely set in."

Ellie rose. "You've had two very hectic nights since you got here. This wasn't probably what you were expecting."

As he covered the distance to the foyer, he stifled another yawn before she thought it was her company. Because that was the furthest from the truth. If he wasn't so exhausted from months of nonstop work and traveling over a day to get home, he could spend hours trying to get to know Ellie St. James. And he had a feeling he wouldn't even begin to understand the woman.

He started up the stairs and she continued walking toward the dining room and kitchen area. "You're not coming upstairs?"

She peered back over her shoulder. "Not until I've checked the house again and made sure we're locked up as tight as we can be."

He rotated toward her. "Do you need company?"

Her chuckle peppered the air. "I've been doing this for a long time. It's second nature. Always know the terrain around you. In this case, this house. If I have to move around it in the dark, I need to know the layout."

"I never thought about that. I'm glad Winnie has you. See you bright and early tomorrow."

"Good night."

The smile that curved her lips zapped him. He mounted the stairs with that picture etched into his mind. He had grown up in this house. Could he move around it if the power went off and not run into every piece of furniture? Her skill set was very different from his. He could leave and be assured Winnie was in good hands.

That conclusion didn't set well with him. It niggled him as he got into bed, and it stayed with him all night.

After securing the house, Ellie ascended to the second floor. Walking toward her bedroom, she paused outside Winnie's room and pressed her ear against the door. Silence greeted her. She continued to hers two doors down. She couldn't shake the feeling they were vulnerable even with the deputy outside.

She immediately crossed the window that overlooked the front of the property. She studied the parked patrol car, glimpsing the man sitting in the front seat. She didn't leave her welfare or a client's to others. She hadn't vetted the deputy. She didn't even know him.

That thought clinched her decision. She went to her bed and gathered up a blanket and pillow then headed for the hallway. Outside Winnie's room, she spread her armload out on the floor then settled down for the night, fitting her gun close to her. This accommodation was four-star compared to some she'd had in the army.

She was a light sleeper, and anyone who wanted Winnie would have to go over her to get her client. She fell asleep with that knowledge.

Only to have someone jostle her shoulder hours later.

She gripped her gun. Her eyes inched open to find Colt stooping over her.

He leaned toward her ear and whispered, "I don't want to disturb Winnie, but Rod is gone. He's not in the car and hasn't been for a while now."

Chapter Five

Ellie was already on her feet, slipping on her shoes as she moved toward the stairs. "Stay here. It might be nothing but stretching his legs."

As she crept down the steps, avoiding the ones that creaked, only the light from the hallway illuminating her path, her eyes began to adjust to the darkness swallowing her at the bottom of the staircase. She saw the red glow on the security keypad across from her.

Before going outside to search for the deputy, she crept through the rooms on the first floor, using the moonlight streaming through the upper part of the windows that weren't draped. When she reached the kitchen, she had to switch on a light to inspect the area and check the back door.

When she returned to the foyer, she flipped

on the light and punched the alarm off then went to the bottom of the steps. "Colt."

He appeared at the railing overlooking the foyer.

"I'm going outside and resetting the alarm. Don't leave there."

"You shouldn't go by yourself."

"I need you to stay there. Don't follow me. Understand?"

He nodded, but his jaw clamped in a hard line.

Ellie set the alarm, hurried toward the front door and slipped outside. She examined the patrol car, still empty. Rod's hat sat on the passenger's seat. That was the only evidence the man had been in the vehicle.

For the second time that night she made her way toward the west side of the property. Had the mountain lion returned and somehow got inside the fence? Earlier they had patched it the best they could. Now she noticed the rope they had tied across the opening had been cut and the fence had been parted again. Alert, she inspected the blackness beyond the property. Her eyes were fully adjusted to the dark, but a good pair of night-vision goggles would have been preferable. She swung around slowly, searching every tree and bush.

Something big lay on the ground near a group of firs. She snuck toward it. The closer she came the more sure she was that it was a body. From the size, probably a man. The body lay still, curled on his side, his face away from her. Was it the deputy? Was he dead?

Removing her small flashlight from her pocket, she increased her pace as well as her alertness in case this was a trap. Someone had cut those ropes.

The person on the ground groaned and rolled over. He tried to sit up and collapsed back. Another moan escaped him as Ellie reached his side.

"Rod? Are you okay?"

"Someone…hit me over the head." He lifted his hand to his hair and yelped when he touched his scalp. Blood covered his fingers.

"Why were you out here?"

"I heard something. I came to see what it was and found one of the dogs lying under the thick brush." He pointed beneath some large holly bushes. "The next thing I knew, I was hit and going down." He struggled to sit up.

Ellie helped him. "Take it easy. I'm phoning this in."

After she placed a call to the sheriff's office, Rod asked, "Is the dog gone?"

Using her small flashlight, Ellie inspected the bushes. "There's no dog here."

"There was a while ago. Its whimpering is what drew me."

"Whoever hit you must have taken the dog. The ropes on the fence were cut and the hole opened up again."

"They came back for the third dog?"

"I guess. Why do you say 'they'?"

"I don't know. It could have been one person or several. The dog weighed sixty or seventy pounds, so one person could have carried it, I guess."

"Or dragged it." She thought of the boot prints, about a size nine in a men's shoe, which meant probably a man of medium height or a large woman. "Can you walk back to the house?"

"Yes. I just need to take it slow."

Putting her arm around him, she assisted him to his feet. "Okay?"

"Yeah, except for a walloping headache."

She checked her watch. "Backup should be here soon."

"I didn't see that dog last night, but it was hidden by the holly bushes. I've got to admit I didn't think a dog was still here. I should have searched more thoroughly." He touched his forehead. "I've learned my lesson."

"It's only an hour or so to sunrise. We can search the whole grounds more thoroughly then."

"Why did whoever took the dogs come back for one of them? That was risky."

"Can't answer that." Although she had an idea. Last night Winnie had been extremely upset about the missing dogs. They had been special to her husband. So the person behind taking the animals might have had two reasons: to hurt the security around Winnie and to hurt her personally. "It does mean someone was watching the house for the right moment to come back."

"Except that I got to the dog before they could."

"It's looking that way."

The deputy gripped the railing as he mounted the steps to the front deck. "Does the sheriff know?"

"Probably."

Before she could unlock the door, Colt opened it. He took one look at Rod and stepped aside to let them inside. "What happened?"

Winnie hurried across the foyer, taking hold of the young man. "Come into the kitchen. Let me clean this gash."

"Ma'am, I'll be okay."

"Not until you see a doctor, and it still needs

to be cleaned up. I have a first-aid kit in the kitchen." Winnie tugged the man forward.

Colt stood in Ellie's way. "What happened?"

She shut and locked the door, then faced him. "He heard a sound coming from the west side of the property and went to check it out. When he found one of your dogs on the ground under some bushes, he was hit over the head."

"One of our dogs wasn't taken?"

"It has been now, or at least I think it has. The dog was gone when I got there. The ropes were cut and the fence opened back up."

"Maybe there's another dog on the grounds?"

"In a couple of hours when it's daylight, we can search more thoroughly and see."

"We'd probably better go rescue Rod. My grandmother can get carried away with a cut or gash. Once she wrapped my calf for a small wound on the back. A bandage would have worked fine."

Ellie had taken a few steps when the doorbell rang. "I'll take care of this. It's probably the sheriff."

After looking through the peephole and seeing Sheriff Quinn, she opened the door. "The deputy should be all right, but he needs to be checked out at the hospital. He was hit over the head. Winnie is tending to him in the kitchen."

As they walked toward the room, Ellie explained where the deputy had been found and about the dog under the bushes.

Winnie glanced up when they entered. Frowning, she finished cleaning up the deputy's head wound. "Someone has stolen my dogs. Come on my property. Threatened me. And now hurt your deputy. I hardly see you, and in less than six hours you've been at my house twice. Neither a social call."

"I have one deputy outside right now and another on his way. Should be here any minute." He turned to Rod. "He can take you to the hospital. Get that head injury examined by the doc."

"Fine by me, but I want to work on this case. When this person came after me, he made it personal." Rod slowly stood and smiled at Winnie. "Thank you, ma'am, for seeing to me."

"Dear, I'm so sorry. You take care of yourself, and you're welcome back here anytime."

Before the sheriff followed his deputy from the room, he said, "If it's okay with you, Mrs. Winfield, I'd like to stay until sunrise and then thoroughly search the grounds."

"Of course. I'll get some coffee on and fix something for breakfast. I have a feeling we'll all need our energy for the day to come." Winnie washed her hands at the sink, then began making some coffee.

"I'll be back as soon as I see to Rod and post

my other deputy. We need to discuss who would do this to you, Mrs. Winfield."

After the sheriff left, Winnie finished with the coffee. With her back to them, she grasped the counter on both sides of her and lowered her head.

"Winnie, are you okay?" Colt asked, coming to his grandmother's side and laying his hand on her shoulder.

The woman straightened from the counter, turned and inhaled a deep breath. "I will be once we find this person. If we get a ransom demand for the dogs, I'll pay it. I want them back. But what if…" Her bottom lip quivered, and she bit down on it.

"We'll do everything we can to get your pets back. I know how much they mean to you."

"I remember all the walks your granddad and I took with our dogs. It was our special time together. I think it was what helped me bounce back from my heart attack."

Colt embraced Winnie. "I'm not going back to the ship until this whole situation is resolved. Your safety means everything to me."

Winnie's eyes glistened. "That means so much to me. You're my only family now."

Behind her Ellie heard footsteps approaching the kitchen. She turned around, her hand on her gun in case it wasn't the sheriff returning. But when he came into the room, she dropped her arm to her side.

"Just in time for some coffee, Sheriff." Winnie stepped away from Colt and busied herself taking four mugs from the cabinet. "If I remember correctly you take yours black."

"Yes, I sure do."

Winnie poured the brew into the mugs then passed them out. "I've been trying to think of anyone who would do this to me. I can't at the moment."

"Let's all sit and talk this out. Sometimes that helps."

Ellie took a chair next to Colt while Sheriff Quinn and Winnie sat across from her. "Who have you fired recently?" she asked.

"No one." Her eyebrows scrunched together. "Well, I haven't personally. Harold and the human resources department handle those kind of things. There are days I don't even go into the office. I prefer working here. That's why I have a fully stocked lab in the basement."

"So you can't think of any disgruntled employees?" The sheriff blew on his coffee then took a sip. "Let's say in the past year."

Her head down, Winnie massaged her fingertips into her forehead. "You need to get a list from Harold. There have only been a few people

I know personally who have left the company in the past year or so."

"Who?" Sheriff Quinn withdrew a small pad along with a pen from his front shirt pocket.

"About a year ago one of the chemists working with me. I wasn't aware of this problem, but two different female employees in the lab accused him of sexual harassment. Glamour Sensations has always had a strict policy against it. Harold fired Dr. Ben Parker. He was difficult to work with but a brilliant chemist. When he came to me and complained, I supported Harold's decision. Frankly, I told him I was disappointed in him and..." Winnie averted her head and stared at the blinds over the window near the table.

"What else?" Colt slid his hand across the table and cupped his grandmother's.

"He said some ugly things to me, mostly directed at Harold and the company rather than at me. I will not repeat them." Squaring her shoulders, she lifted her chin.

The sheriff wrote down the man's name on the pad. "Okay, Winnie. We have one we can check on. Anyone else?"

"The only other who I had any contact with is the driver I used to have before my current one." She paused for a long moment. "I guess I was directly responsible for his dismissal. He came to work one day drunk. I knew he'd been having marital troubles so I was willing to give him a second chance. We all need those, but Harold was adamant that we don't. In the end I agreed with Harold."

"Harold was right. You can't be driven around by a person who has been drinking. What's his name?"

"Jerry Olson."

"Any more?" The sheriff took another drink of his coffee.

Winnie shook her head. "None. But there are a lot of departments I don't have any interaction with."

"How about someone who's been passed over for a raise or promotion?" Ellie cradled her mug between her cold hands. "This person doesn't necessarily have to be gone from the company."

"Well…" Winnie patted her hair down, her mouth pursed. "We did have several candidates to be the spokesperson for Endless Youth. Christy actually wasn't in the running. I'm the one who decided she would be perfect. She might not be considered beautiful by a model's standard, but she conveyed what I wanted to communicate to the everyday woman. There were two young women before Christy who were in the final running for the position. Mary Ann Witlock and Lara Ulrich. I suppose neither one was happy when they weren't picked. They don't work for Glamour Sensations. Lara Ulrich lives in Denver, and Mary Ann Witlock lives in Bakersville. Several members of her family work for Glamour Sensations, but she works as a waitress at the restaurant not far from the company's main office."

The sheriff jotted down the additional names. "If you think of anyone else, give me a call. I'll be meeting with Harold and the police chief in Bakersville to see who they're looking at."

"Have you all thought this could be simply a kidnapping of my dogs?" Winnie asked. "They are valuable. But even more so to me. Anyone who knows me knows that."

Ellie nodded. "True, but they're even more valuable to you because you care for them so much. That could be the reason the person decided to steal them." She downed the last swallow of her coffee and went to get the pot and bring it back to the table. "Anyone else want some more?"

Colt held up his mug, as did the sheriff. Winnie shook her head.

The sheriff closed his notepad. "After I look around, I'll go back to the office and track down these people."

"How's an omelet for breakfast?" Winnie

left her nearly untouched drink and crossed to the refrigerator.

"Wait until Linda comes to prepare breakfast." Colt pulled the blind to let in the soft light of dawn. "When she sees all the cars out front, she'll be here early."

"No, I need to keep busy. Besides, I don't get to cook like I used to. Thomas loved my omelets. Now to remember how to make them."

"I'll help."

Colt shifted his attention to Ellie. "You cook?"

"Yes, some. I have to eat so I learned how."

One of his eyebrow arched. "A bodyguard who can cook. A woman of many talents."

"I'd love your help," Winnie said. "Be useful, Colt, and take this cup of coffee to the deputy outside."

He passed Ellie as he left with a mug and whispered, "Watch her. She once almost set the kitchen on fire. That's why Granddad insisted she hire Linda to cook."

"I heard that, young man. At least I don't go outside barefoot in winter."

Ellie slanted a look toward Colt as he left. In the doorway he glanced back and locked gazes with her. Then he winked.

Heat scored Ellie's cheeks. She'd never been around a family like the Winfields. She would have loved having the caring and the give-and-take between her and her mother. What would it have been like to grow up in a loving family? She could only imagine.

Ellie watched the last workmen leave, the black iron gates at the end of the drive shutting closed after the truck passed through the entrance to the estate. The sun disappeared completely below the western mountains, throwing a few shadows across the landscape. She surveyed the nearly fortified property, her muscles still tense from all the activity that had occurred during the day.

"What do you think?" Colt asked, coming up behind her.

"I'd rather have been in the lab with Winnie than out here supervising."

"The sheriff put a deputy on the door to the lab. Your expertise was needed making sure everything went in correctly. Winnie needed her security system updated even without the threat to her."

"I agree. She thinks being isolated keeps her protected. On the contrary, that makes her more vulnerable." She threw him a grin. "I just hate it when I need to be in two places at once. But you're right. I needed to keep an eye on the workers and the job they were doing. After tomorrow I'll breathe even easier."

"When they mount the cameras and put in the monitoring station?"

"Yes. The only one up and running right now is at the front gate. I'm glad Winnie agreed to let us use that small room off the kitchen for the monitoring station. It's a good location. Even at night we'll be able to tell what is happening outside on the grounds."

"That would have been nice last night." Colt lounged against the railing, his gaze fixed on her.

The intensity in his look lured her nearer. It took all her willpower to stay where she was. "I'm hoping the electrified fence will keep people and large animals away. If someone tries to circumvent the power on the fence, the company monitoring it will notify the house. The jolt won't kill, but it will discourage someone or something from touching it."

"Tomorrow the two guard dogs from the trainer in Denver will arrive, but with the fence up and running and the new security system for the house, we should be all right."

He hadn't phrased it as a question, but his furrowed forehead indicated his lingering doubts. "No place can be one hundred percent safe, but this will be a vast improvement over yesterday. I wasn't sure how much they would accomplish today, but it helped that Winnie could afford to pay for a rush job."

"I got through to the *Kaleidoscope* and told them I have a family emergency. Just when you think you're indispensable, you find out they'll be all right without you. But then I figure you don't feel that way too much in your job. I know Winnie needs you. Yesterday proved that." He snapped his fingers. "I almost forgot. The sheriff called. He's on his way from Bakersville to give us an update on the people they're checking out."

"So he'll be here about the time Harold arrives. He wants us to have photos of the people Winnie mentioned and some he thought of. He wants us to convince Winnie not to attend the lighting of the Christmas tree in Bakersville tomorrow night."

Colt straightened, his movement bringing him a step closer. "I'll give it my best shot, but I don't think Winnie will change her mind. Bakersville is honoring Granddad and her at the tree lighting for all the work they've done for the town. That's important to her. Bakersville has been her home a long time since she married my granddad and came to live here."

"As important as her life?"

"My grandmother can be a stubborn woman."

"Tell me about it. She didn't want the deputy

in the basement. She thought he could sit in the kitchen where he would be more comfortable. I told her that workers will have to come down there and that I can't follow every worker around. The deputy stands at the door to her lab or inside with her."

"I know she balked at that. She doesn't even like me in there. Anybody in the lab is a distraction, and she is determined to complete the project in time. She believes it's tied to who is after her. She thinks it's a competitor."

"That's still a possibility. The P.I. is looking into that. Maybe Harold will have some information."

Colt nodded his head toward the gate. "That's his car now and it looks like the sheriff is behind him."

"Nothing is assured until I check the monitor," Ellie said as she hurried inside and to the small room off the kitchen.

She examined the TV that showed the feed from the front gate. Harold waved at the camera. After clicking him through, she observed the Lexus as it passed the lower camera that gave a view of anyone in the vehicle. It appeared Harold was alone. Then she did the same thing with the sheriff.

When she glanced up, Colt stood in the doorway, his arms straight at his side while his gaze took in the bank of TV monitors. "We need someone to be in here 24/7 until this is over with."

"I agree, and I'm hoping you'll help me convince your grandmother of that in a few minutes."

"So you gathered the forces to help you?"

"Yes. She may be upset with Harold for not telling her sooner, but she trusts him. And she respects the sheriff."

"You are sly, Miss St. James, and I'm glad you are. In a week's time you have gotten to know Winnie well."

"I got a head start. On the plane ride here, I studied a file Harold provided me on her. From what he wrote, I could tell how much he cares about her. In army intelligence, I had to learn quick how to read people."

He closed the space between them. "That means you can't be fooled?"

"I'd be a fool to think that."

His chuckle resonated through the air. "Good answer. I like you, Ellie St. James."

The small room seemed to shrink as she looked at the dimple in his left cheek, the laugh lines at the corners of his eyes. She scrambled to form some kind of reply that would make sense. But as his soft gaze roamed over her features it left a tingling path where it touched as if he'd brushed his fingers over her face.

The doorbell sounded, breaking the mood.

"I'll get Winnie," he murmured in a husky voice.

She stepped to the side and rushed past him to the foyer. Her heartbeat pounded against her rib cage, and her breath was shallow as she peered through the peephole then opened the door to Harold and the sheriff.

"Colt's gone to get his grandmother," Ellie told them. "She wanted to be included in the update."

"How's she holding up?" Harold asked as they made their way into the living room.

"Fine, Harold." Winnie answered before Ellie could. "Worried? Is that why you didn't answer your private line today when I called?"

With his cheeks flushed, the CFO of Glamour Sensations faced Winnie coming down the hall. "I've been busy working with the police chief, to make sure we have a thorough list of people who could possibly be angry with you."

The older woman's usual warm blue eyes frosted. "I've always tried to treat people fairly. How many are we talking about?"

"Including the ones you gave the sheriff, in the past two years, ten."

Her taut bearing drooped a little. "That many? I've never intentionally hurt someone."

"It might not be you per se but your company. Tomorrow I'm going to look back five years."

"Why so far back?" Winnie looked from Harold to the sheriff, her delicate eyebrows crunching together.

"It's probably no one that far back, but I'd rather cover all our bases. It's better to be safe than—"

Winnie held up her hand. "Don't say it. It's been a long day. It was nearly impossible to think clearly with all the racket going on earlier. This may throw me behind a day or so. Give me the facts, and then I need to go back to the lab to finish up what should have been completed two hours ago." She came into the room as far as the wingback chair but remained standing behind it.

"Winnie, the workmen will be gone by midafternoon tomorrow. They're mounting cameras all over the estate and activating the monitoring system. The only one right now that works is the front gate." Ellie took a seat, hoping her client would follow suit. The pale cast to Winnie's face and her lackluster eyes worried Ellie.

Sheriff Quinn cleared his throat. "We've narrowed the list down to the three most likely with two maybes." He withdrew his pad. "The first one is Lara Ulrich. Although she lives in Denver, that's only an hour away, and she has been spotted in Bakersville this past month, visiting her mother. I discovered she's moving back home because she can't get enough work to support herself in Denver. Jerry Olson is working when he can but mostly he's living off his aunt, who is losing her patience with him. He's been vocal about you not giving him that second chance you're known for. The last is someone Harold brought to my attention. Steve Fairchild is back in town."

Winnie gasped.

Chapter Six

Winnie leaned into the back of the chair, clutching it. "When?"

"A few weeks ago," Harold said, getting up and moving to Winnie.

Ellie glanced at Colt. A tic in his jaw twitched. She slid her hand to his on the couch and he swung his attention to her as she mouthed, "Who is that?"

He bent toward her and whispered, "She blamed him for causing Granddad's death."

"Why is this the first time I've heard about him?"

"Right after my grandfather died he left Bakersville to work overseas."

"Because I drove him out of town," Winnie said in a raw voice, finally taking a seat. "I said some horrible things to the man in public that I regretted when I came to my right mind." A sheen of tears shone in her eyes. "I wronged him and thought I would never have a chance to apologize. I must go see him."

"No." Colt's hand beneath Ellie's on the couch fisted. "Not when someone is after you. Not when that someone could be him."

Winnie stiffened, gripping both arms of the chair. "Young man, I will do what I have to. I will not let this wrong go on any longer. I need to apologize—in public. My words and actions were what caused people to make his life so miserable he left town. Wasn't it bad enough that Thomas had fired him that day he died?"

"I need you to tell me what happened." Ellie rose, her nerves jingling as if she felt they were close to an answer.

"Steve Fairchild messed up a huge account for Glamour Sensations. Thomas lost a lot of sleep over what to do about him. That day he fired Steve, Thomas stayed late trying to repair the damage the man had done to the company. I blamed Steve Fairchild for my husband falling asleep behind the wheel. That was grief talking. I now realize Thomas made the choice to drive home when he could have stayed at his office and slept on the couch."

Harold pounded the arm of his chair and sat forward. "Winnie, the man was at fault. We took a hard knock when that client walked away from our company. It took us a year to get back what we lost. You only said what half the town felt, and then on top of everything, he dared to come to Thomas's funeral. You were not in the wrong."

Winnie pressed her lips together. For a long moment silence filled the room. "This is the last I'm going to say on the subject. I owe the man an apology, and I intend to give it to him." She swept her attention to the sheriff. "What about Mary Ann Witlock?"

"I'm still looking for her. She's not been seen for a week. She told her neighbor she was going to Texas to see a boyfriend. That's all I've been able to find out so far."

"And you don't think Dr. Ben Parker is a threat?"

"No, he's in a nursing home in Denver."

"He is? Why?"

"He had a severe stroke. He can't walk and has trouble talking."

"Oh, dear. I need to add him to my prayer list."

"He wouldn't leave the young women in his lab alone," Harold muttered, scowling.

Winnie tilted up her chin. "That doesn't mean I shouldn't pray for him. You and I have never seen eye to eye on praying for people regardless."

Listening to the older woman gave Ellie something to think about. She was a Christian, but was her faith strong? Could she forgive her mother for her neglect or the bullies that made her brother's life miserable? She didn't know if she had that in her, especially when she remembered Toby coming home crying with a bloodied face.

"We'll continue to delve into these people's lives. I'm just glad the police chief is handling it quietly and personally," Harold said with a long sigh. "He's trying to track down how the letters came to your office. There was no postmark. He's reviewing security footage, but there are a lot of ways to put a letter in the interoffice mail at your company. Some of them aren't on the camera."

"Fine." Winnie slapped her hands on her thighs and started to push up from her seat. "I've got a few more hours of—"

"Grandma, we have something else we need to talk to you about." Colt's words stopped her.

Ellie noticed the woman's eyebrows shoot up.

"Grandma?" Winnie asked. "Is there something else serious you've been keeping from me? You never call me Grandma." Her gaze flitted from one person to the next.

Ellie approached Winnie. "I'm strongly rec-ommending that you not go to the lighting of the Christmas tree tomorrow night."

"I'm going, so each of you better accept that. Knowing you, Harold, you've hired security. I wouldn't be surprised if every other person in the crowd was security. I won't let this person rob me of all my little pleasures." She stood, her arms stiff at her sides. "Just make sure they don't stand out."

Evidently Colt was not satisfied. "Grandma—"

"Don't 'Grandma' me. I will not give in to this person totally. I'm already practically a prisoner in this house, and after tomorrow, this place will be as secure as a prison." She marched toward the exit. "I'll be in my lab. Have Linda bring my dinner to me. I'm eating alone tonight."

Quiet ruled until the basement door slammed shut.

"That worked well," Colt mumbled and caught Ellie's look. "What do you suggest?"

"Short of locking her in her room, nothing. I'd say strengthen the security and pray. I won't leave her side. Harold, have you found a few people to monitor the TVs around the clock here at the house?"

"Yes. With the police chief and Sheriff Quinn's help, I have four who are willing to start tomorrow. One is a deputy and two are police officers. They need extra money. My fourth one is the retired police chief. He's bored and needs something to do. They will be discreet."

"Perfect." Although the police chief and sheriff vouched for the men, she would have her employer do a background check on them. She'd learned to double-check everything. "I'd like a list of their names."

The sheriff jotted them down on a piece of paper. "I personally know all these men, and they will do a good job."

"That's good. Did you discover what kind of vehicle could have left those tire tracks?"

"The tire is pretty common for a SUV, so probably not a truck."

"What was in the dart?" Ellie held her breath, hoping it wasn't a poison. Winnie still thought there was a chance to get her dogs back.

Sheriff Quinn rose. "A tranquilizer. We're checking vets and sources where it can be purchased. But that will take time."

Time we might not have.

After Ellie escorted the two men to the front door then locked it when they left, she turned to see Colt in the foyer, staring at her. The scent of roasted chicken spiced the air. Her stomach rumbled. "I just realized all I had today was breakfast."

"It looks like it will be just you and me tonight."

The sudden cozy picture of them sitting before a roaring fire sharing a delicious dinner stirred feelings deep inside her she'd fought to keep pushed down. She'd purposely picked this life as a bodyguard to help others but also to keep her distance from people. She was more of an observer, not a participant. When she had participated, she'd gotten hurt—first with her family and later when she became involved with Greg, a man she had dated seriously who had lied to her.

Colt walked toward her, a crooked grin on his face. "We have to eat. We might as well do it together and get to know each other. It looks like we'll be working together to protect Winnie."

"Working together? I don't think so. I'm the bodyguard, not you. You're her grandson. You are emotionally involved. That can lead to mistakes, problems."

He moved into her personal space, suddenly crowding her even though he was a couple of feet away. "Being emotionally involved will drive me to do what I need to protect my grandmother. Feelings aren't the enemy."

They aren't? Ellie had her doubts. She'd felt for her mother, her brother and Greg, and ended up hurt, a little bit of herself lost. "Feelings can get in the way of doing your job."

"It's dinner, Ellie. That's all. In the kitchen."

"I know that. I'm checking the house one more time, then I'll be in there to eat." She started to leave.

He stepped into her path. "I want to make it clear. I will be involved with guarding Winnie. That's not negotiable."

She met the hard, steely look in his eyes. "Everything is negotiable." Then she skirted around him and started her room-by-room search, testing the windows and looking in places a person could hide. She'd counted the workmen as they'd left, but she liked to double-check.

As she passed through the house, she placed a call to her employer. "I need you to investigate some law enforcement officers who are helping with monitoring the cameras I've had installed around the estate. The sheriff and police chief vetted them."

Kyra Hunt laughed. "But you don't know if you can trust them?"

"No. You taught me well. I can remember a certain police officer being dirty on a case you took."

"I've already looked into Sheriff Quinn and the police chief. Nothing I can find sends up a red flag."

Like the background checks Kyra did on Harold Jefferson, Linda and Doug Miller, and Christy Boland. She knew nothing was completely foolproof, but she would be a fool if she didn't have these background checks done on people who came in close contact with Winnie. After she gave the four names to Kyra, she said, "Also look into Colt Winfield. He came home unexpectedly and is now staying."

"Mrs. Winfield's grandson? Do you suspect him?"

"No, not really, but then I can't afford to be wrong."

"I'll get back to you with what I find."

When Ellie finished her call, she walked toward the kitchen, the strong aroma of spices and roast chicken making her mouth water.

"Linda, I'll take care of the dishes. Go home," Colt said as Ellie came into the room.

Linda nodded. "I imagine Doug is asleep. Today was an early one, and with all that's been going on, he didn't have much chance to even sit." She removed her apron and hung it up on a peg. "Winnie said she'll bring up her dinner tray later."

Ellie crossed to the back door and locked it

after the housekeeper left. She watched out the window as the woman hurried across the yard toward the guesthouse where she and her husband lived. "I haven't had a chance to tell her today that any guests she has will have to go through me first. I'll do that first thing tomorrow." She pivoted, her gaze connecting with Colt's.

"We talked about it. She's fine meeting anyone she needs in town for the time being."

"Just so long as her car is inspected when she comes back."

Surprise flashed across her face. "You think Linda might be involved?"

"No, but what if someone managed to hide in her car? Then when she drove onto the property they would be inside without us knowing. It's necessary until we know how the new dogs are going to work out."

"You have to think of everything."

"My clients depend on it. As we speak, I'm having the men who are going to monitor the security system vetted by my employer. Nothing is foolproof, but there are some procedures I can put in place to make this house safer, so Winnie won't have to worry about walking around her own home. I've had everyone who comes into close contact with Winnie on a regular basis checked out."

"Harold?

"Yes, just because he hired me doesn't make him not a suspect."

"Me?" Colt pulled out a chair for her to sit in at the kitchen table set for two.

"Yes, even you."

"I'm her grandson!"

"I know, but some murders have been committed by family members."

He took the chair across from her. "Do you trust anyone?" he asked in a tightly controlled voice.

"I'm paid to distrust."

"How about when you aren't working? Do you go around distrusting everyone?"

"I trust God."

"No one else?"

Ellie picked up the fork and speared a slice of roasted chicken. Who did she trust? The list was short. "How about you? Who do you trust?"

His intense gaze snared hers. "I trust you to protect my grandmother."

"Then why are you wanting to do my job?"

"Because I trust myself to protect my grandmother, too. Isn't two better than one?"

"Not necessarily."

After he scooped some mashed potatoes onto his plate he passed her the bowl. "You never answered my question about who you trust."

"I know." Her hand gripping her fork tight, she dug into her dinner. His question disturbed her because she didn't have a ready answer—a list of family and friends she could say she trusted. Could she trust Colt?

The chilly temperature and the low clouds in the dark night promised snow when they arrived at the tree lighting. Ellie buttoned her short coat and checked her gun before she slid from the front passenger seat of the SUV. "Winnie, wait until I open your door."

While Colt exited the car, Ellie helped his grandmother from the backseat. The whole time Ellie scanned the crowd in the park next to City Hall, her senses alert for anything out of the ordinary. Lights blazed from the two-story building behind the tree and from the string of colored lights strung from pole to pole along the street, but too many of the townspeople were shrouded in darkness where the illumination didn't reach.

Ellie flanked Winnie on the right side while Colt took the left one. "Ready?" she asked.

"I see Harold waving to us from the platform near the Christmas tree." Colt guided his grandmother toward Glamour Sensations' CFO.

"No one said anything about you standing on a platform," Ellie said. The idea that Winnie would be up above the crowd—a better target—bothered Ellie. She continued her search of the faces in the mob, looking for any of the ones the police were looking into as the possible threat to Winnie.

"Oh, yes. I have to give a speech before I flip the switch. I'll keep it short, dear."

Ellie wasn't sure Winnie took the threat against her as seriously as she should. "How about you skip the speech and go straight to turning on the lights so we can leave?"

Winnie paused and shifted toward Ellie. "I've lived a long, good life. If I go to my maker tonight, then so be it."

"Winnie," Colt said in a sharp voice that reached the people around them. They all turned to watch them. Leaning toward his grandmother, he murmured, "I'm not ready to give you up. I'd care if something happened to you."

Winnie patted his arm. "I know. But I want you two to realize I have a peace about all of this. That doesn't mean I will fire Ellie—" she tossed a look toward Ellie "—because I won't give the person after me an easy target. But, as I'm sure she knows, there is only so much you all can do. The only one who can protect me is the Lord."

"But you know He uses others to do His bidding. I fall into that category. If I tell you to do something, just do it. No questions asked, okay?" Ellie wished she could get Winnie to take this whole situation more seriously.

"Yes, my dear."

"If I see a threat in the crowd, I'm going to get you out of here. Then later you can chalk it up to a crazy assistant getting overzealous in her job if you need to spin it for the press. Let's get this over with."

Up on the platform as Winnie approached the podium and the cheering crowd quieted, Colt whispered to Ellie, "You make this sound like we've come for a root canal."

"How about several? I don't like this at all." She gestured toward one area of the park that was particularly dark. "Why couldn't they have the lighting of the tree during the daytime?"

Her gaze latched onto a man in the front row reaching into his coat pocket. Ellie stiffened and put her hand into her own pocket, grasping her weapon. But the guy pulled out a cell and turned it off.

Five minutes later when Winnie completed her short speech thanking Bakersville for the honor to Thomas and her for naming the park after them, she stepped over to flip the first switch. Suddenly the lights went out in City Hall and the only ones that illuminated the area were the string of colorful lights along the streets and around the park. Next Winnie flipped the switch for the lights on the twelve-foot Christmas tree and their colorful glow lit the area.

"That's why it's at nighttime."

The tickle of Colt's whisper by her ear shot a bolt of awareness through Ellie. Her pulse rate accelerated, causing a flush of heat on her face. Someone in the crowd began singing "Joy to the World" and everyone joined in, including Colt and Winnie. Ellie sang but never took her attention from the people surrounding Winnie. Harold had said he would have people in plainclothes scattered throughout the attendees in addition to the police visible in the throng.

Ellie moved closer, intending to steer Winnie back to the SUV. But before she could grasp her elbow, women, men and children swamped Winnie.

"Thank you for what you've done for Bakersville," one lady said.

Another person shook Winnie's hand. "When the economy was down, you didn't lay off anyone at the company. We appreciate that."

After five long minutes of the same kind of praises, Ellie stepped to Winnie's right while Colt took up his position on the left.

Winnie grinned. "Thank you all. Bakersville is important to me. It's my home."

People parted to allow Winnie through the

crowd. Suddenly a medium-built man stepped into Winnie's path. Ellie inched closer to Winnie while she gripped her weapon.

Winnie smiled. "I'm glad to see you, Mr. Fairchild. I heard you were in town."

"Yeah. Is there a problem with me being here?" He pulled himself up straight, his shoulders back.

"No, on the contrary, I meant it. I'm glad I ran into you." She raised her voice. "I wanted to apologize to you for my behavior right after Thomas died. I was wrong. I hope you'll accept my apology."

The man's mouth dropped open. The tension in his stance eased. "I—I—"

"I would certainly understand if you don't, but I hope you'll find it in your heart to—"

"I made mistakes, too," Steve Fairchild mumbled. Then he ducked his head and hurried off.

"Let's go, Winnie," Ellie said and guided her client toward the car.

The closer they got to the SUV the faster Ellie's pace became. Her nape tingled; her breath caught in her lungs. The person behind the threats was here somewhere—she felt it in her bones. Possibly Steve Fairchild, in spite of how the encounter had turned out. Not until Winnie was safe in the backseat and Colt was pulling out of the parking space did Ellie finally exhale.

"I thought that went very well, especially with Steve Fairchild, and nothing happened at the lighting of the tree," Winnie said from the backseat.

We're not at your house yet. Ellie kept that thought to herself, but her gaze continually swept the landscape and the road before and behind the SUV.

Winnie continued to comment on the event. "The Christmas tree this year was beautiful. Not that it isn't every year, but they seemed to have more decorations and lights on it. You were here last Christmas, Colt. Don't you think it was bigger and better?"

Ellie tossed a quick glance at Colt. In the beam of an oncoming car, she glimpsed his set jaw, his focus totally on the road ahead.

"I guess so. I never thought about it."

"Isn't that just like a man, Ellie?"

"Yes, but I've found a lot of people don't note their surroundings unless there's a reason." Ellie couldn't help but notice that Winnie hadn't said much on the ride down the mountain, but now she wanted to chitchat. That was probably her nerves talking. "You'll be all right, Winnie. I won't let anything happen to you."

"I know that. I'm not worried."

"Then why are you talking so much?" Tension threaded through Colt's question.

"I'm relieved nothing happened and pleased by the kindness of the people of Bakersville. I even got my chance to apologize to Mr. Fairchild in public. I wish I could have stayed longer. I probably should call the mayor tomorrow and apologize that I couldn't linger at the end. I usually do."

Behind the SUV a car sped closer. Ellie couldn't tell the make of the vehicle from the glare of the headlights.

"I see it." Colt slowed down.

The car accelerated and passed them on a straight part of the winding road up the mountain. The Ford Focus increased its distance between them and disappeared around a curve. Ellie twisted to look behind them. A dark stretch of highway greeted her inspection.

She sat forward, her hand going to her gun. She took it out and laid it on her lap.

"Expecting trouble?" Colt asked.

Although it was dark inside the SUV, with only a few dashboard lights, Ellie felt the touch of his gaze when he turned his head toward her. "Always. That's what keeps me alert."

"Oh, my goodness, Ellie," Winnie exclaimed. "That would be hard to do all the time. When do you relax, my dear?"

"When I'm not working."

"I noticed you slept outside my bedroom again last night. You can't be getting rest."

Ellie looked back at Winnie. "Now that the security system is totally functioning and someone is monitoring it at night, I can go back to my room. But I'm a light sleeper on the job whether in a bed or on the floor in front of a door." After checking behind the SUV, she rotated forward. "You don't need to worry about me."

"Oh, but, my dear, I do. How do you think I'd feel if anything happened to you because of me?"

Again Colt and Ellie exchanged glances. She'd never had a client worry about her. If Harold hadn't hired her, she doubted Winnie would have, even knowing about the threatening letters. That thought chilled her. The woman would have been an easy target for anyone.

As the SUV approached the next S-curve, the one where Winnie's husband went off the cliff, Colt took it slow, leaning forward, intent on the road.

When they made it through without any problem, Winnie blew out a breath. "I hate that part of the road. If I could avoid it and get down the mountain, I would. That's a particularly dangerous curve."

"It's not much farther. Which is good since

they're predicting snow tonight." Colt took the next curve.

Halfway through it Ellie saw the car parked across both lanes of the road. With no place to maneuver around it, Colt slammed on his brakes and Ellie braced for impact.

Chapter Seven

Ellie gasped as the brakes screamed and Colt struggled to keep the vehicle from swerving. She muttered a silent prayer just before they collided with the car across the road. The crashing sound reverberated through the SUV. The impact with the side of the Ford Focus jerked Ellie forward then threw her back. The safety belt cut into her chest, holding her against the seat.

"Are you okay?" Ellie fumbled with her buckle, released it and shoved open the door.

"Yes." Colt swiveled around to look at his grandmother.

"I'm fine," she said from the backseat.

Ellie panned the crash site as she hurried toward the car. She couldn't get to the driver's door because of the SUV so she rounded the back of the vehicle and opened the front passenger's door to look inside. Emptiness mocked her.

She straightened and turned to Colt. "Have Winnie stay inside."

Standing by his car, Colt nodded and went around to Winnie's side.

"No one is in the car. Call it in." Keeping vigilant, Ellie scanned the landscape and then made her way back to the SUV. She stood outside the vehicle.

"He said he was fifteen minutes away," Colt told her from the backseat where he sat next to his grandmother.

"Winnie, would you please get down," Ellie chided. "No sense giving anyone a target to shoot at."

"You think he's out there waiting to shoot me?"

Ellie looked around. "Could be. Someone drove this car here and left it across the road in just the right place for anyone coming around the curve to hit it. If this had been car trouble, where is the driver?"

"Walking to get help?" Winnie's voice quavered.

"But there's no reason to have it stalled across the road like this and not to leave the hazard lights flashing."

When Winnie scooted down on the floor, Colt hovered over her like a human shield.

"No, I'm not going to let you do that. I won't let you be killed in my place. Colt, sit back up."

"No. I won't make it easy for them."

"You're going back to your ship tomorrow." Anger weaved through Winnie's voice.

"We'll talk about this when we're safe at the house."

"Don't placate me. I'm your elder."

Ellie heard the back-and-forth between them and knew the fear they both were experiencing. She had a good douse of it herself. But she planted herself beside the back door, her gun raised against her chest. "Shh, you two. I need to listen."

Not another word came from inside the SUV. Ellie focused on the quiet, occasionally broken by a sound—something scurrying in the underbrush on the side of the road, a sizzling noise from under the hood, an owl's hoot. Finally a siren pierced the night. Its blare grew closer. Ellie smiled. She liked how Sheriff Quinn thought. Let whoever might be out here know that help was nearby. Through the trees on the cliff side, Ellie caught snatches of the red flashing lights as two patrol cars sped up the winding highway toward them. Help would be there in less than two minutes.

Even when the sheriff arrived at the wreck site, Ellie concentrated on her surroundings, not the patrol cars screeching to a halt and the doors slamming shut. Finally she slid a glance toward Sheriff Quinn marching toward her while three of his deputies fanned out.

"Is everyone all right?" The sheriff stopped, reaching out to open the back door.

"Yes, but I need to get Winnie to the estate." Ellie backed up against the SUV. "I don't think anyone is going to do anything now, but she isn't safe out here."

The sheriff pointed to his deputies. "One of you get behind that car. Let's see if we can push it out of the way. Wear gloves. We'll want to pull fingerprints off the steering wheel if possible. Someone left this baby out here." He waved his hand toward the car. "And I intend to find out who did this."

Colt climbed from the backseat, closing his grandmother inside and positioning his body at the door.

While the deputies moved the car off to the side of the road, the sheriff switched on his spotlight, sweeping the area. Ellie followed the beam, delving into the shadows for any sign of someone still hanging around.

Then the sheriff moved his car up along the SUV, rolled down the windows and said, "Winnie needs to get out on this side and into my car. If anyone was here, they'd be along the mountainside, not the cliff side of the highway. It's a sheer drop to the bottom."

"I'll take care of it," Ellie said to Colt. "When Winnie and I are in the sheriff's car, take the front seat."

Colt stepped to the side as Ellie slipped inside the backseat of the SUV, then he shut the door and resumed his position.

"Winnie, did you hear the sheriff?"

"It's hard not to. He was shouting."

"I'm going to follow you out of this car. We'll sit in the back of the patrol car."

"Do I hunch down in there, too?"

"It wouldn't hurt. We don't know what we're up against. Caution is always the best policy."

Winnie crawled across the floor to the other side of the backseat. She gripped the handle and pulled it down. "Here goes." The older woman scrambled out of the SUV and into the patrol car two feet away.

Ellie followed suit, and Colt jumped into the front.

The sheriff gunned his engine, maneuvering up the road with expert precision. "We had a report of a stolen Ford Focus from the parking lot near City Hall. A family came back from watching the tree lighting and found their car gone."

So someone had been at the celebration and decided not to go after Winnie in a crowd. Instead, he chose a dark, lonely stretch of road to cause a wreck. Was that someone Steve Fairchild? He had been at the tree lighting and he'd made a point to see Winnie. Was that his way of taunting her before he made his move?

If Colt hadn't been as alert as he had and his reflexes quick, the crash would have been a lot worse. Ellie peered at Winnie's face. She couldn't see the woman's expression, but she held her body rigid. Tension poured off Winnie.

Ellie felt a strong urge to comfort the woman. "You're almost home."

"Someone hates me that much. We could have gone off the road like…" Her voice melted into the silence.

"We'll find the person." Sheriff Quinn stopped at the main gate to the estate and peered back at Winnie. "This is my top priority. I'm leaving two deputies here, and I'm not going to take no for an answer."

Ellie pushed the remote button to allow them inside. As they headed for the main house, the two dogs followed the car as trained.

"Fine, whatever you think is best," Winnie said, the words laced with defeat.

Ellie covered Winnie's clasped hands in her lap. "If someone was trying to stir memories of your husband's wreck, then he would have picked the S-curve for it to happen. His intent would have been clear if he had done that. There still could be a logical explanation that has nothing to do with you. It could be kids joyriding who got scared and ditched the car."

"Do you really believe that?" Winnie asked, her hands tightening beneath Ellie's.

"It's a possibility. That's all I'm saying. Until I know for sure, I don't rule out anything." But something she said to Winnie nibbled at the edges of her mind. Was there a connection to Winnie's husband somehow? What if he didn't fall asleep at the wheel? What if it had been murder five years ago?

A couple of hours later, Ellie entered the kitchen where the sheriff and Colt sat at the table, drinking coffee and reviewing what had occurred.

"How's Winnie?" Colt walked to the carafe and poured Ellie a cup of the black brew.

She took a deep breath of the aroma. "She's bouncing back. I think the similarity to what happened to her husband is what got her more than anything."

"I agree. It worries me, too. A few threatening letters and cut-up pictures aren't nearly as menacing as trying to re-create the same kind of accident. My first instinct was to swerve and avoid the car. If I'd done that, we could have gone off the cliff." Colt slumped into his chair, releasing a sigh.

Ellie sat beside him. "That has me thinking, Sheriff. Your department handled Thomas Winfield's accident. Are you one hundred percent sure it was an accident?"

"Yes, as sure as you can be. When all this began with Winnie, I reviewed the file. Nothing to indicate he was forced off the road, no skid marks. The tire tracks on the shoulder of the road were from Thomas's car. No one else's. No stalled car like this evening. We checked for drinking and drugs, too. He had no alcohol or drugs in his system."

"He shouldn't have," Colt said. "Granddad didn't drink, and his medicine wouldn't have made him sleepy."

"I know, but there was a report of a car weaving over into the other lane a few miles from where the wreck occurred. The man who reported it honked and the driver of the other car swerved in time to miss him. That person watched that car drive off, and it was going straight, no more weaving. He called it in, anyway. His description wasn't detailed, but what he said did fit your grandfather's car."

"So you're saying in your opinion it was an accident?" Ellie took a large swallow of her coffee.

"Yes. Besides, nothing has happened in five years. Why something now? Why Winnie?"

Colt raked his fingers through his hair. "How in the world do you two sit calmly and talk about this kind of stuff?"

"Because it's good to talk about all the possibilities. Brainstorm theories." The sheriff stood. "Ellie, I'll take another look at the file, but I don't think there's a connection. While you were checking on Winnie, two of my deputies arrived after processing the scene of the wreck. The Ford Focus was towed, and we'll go over it, check for fingerprints in the front seat and door. Maybe something will turn up. Also the SUV was towed to the garage in town to be fixed. I'm posting one deputy inside at the front door and the other at the back. Don't want the two new dogs to mistake them for an intruder."

Ellie started to get up.

Sheriff Quinn waved her down. "I'll send the deputy in here and see myself out."

When he left, Colt looked at her. "Let's go into the den."

Too wired to go to sleep yet, she nodded, topped off her coffee and trailed after Colt.

In the den, he stoked the fire he'd made when they had first come home. Winnie had been cold and sat by it until she'd gone to bed. Ellie observed the strong breadth of his shoulders:

his movements were precise, efficient, like the man. She liked what she saw.

When he sank onto the couch next to her, he picked up his mug and sipped his coffee. "I never thought my brief vacation was going to turn out like this."

"I can imagine. No one plans for this."

He angled so he faced her, his arm slung along the back of the couch. "What if Harold hadn't acted quickly on those letters? What if Winnie's assistant hadn't alerted Harold about the threats? I know Winnie. She would have dismissed it. She wants to think the best of everyone. This could have been totally different, especially tonight."

"We can't think about the what-ifs. It's wasted energy."

"Which is precious right now. At least the house and grounds are secure. Winnie won't be happy seeing the deputies here tomorrow morning. She's worried the press will get hold of the fact that she's been threatened and make a big deal out of it. That could jeopardize the company going public. So far the people involved have remained quiet. That won't last long. I know Harold will have to notify certain people if nothing is solved by Christmas. Maybe that is the point of all of this."

"If the news does go public, that might actually help Winnie. Most of the people in this town love Winnie and will want to help her. Someone might come forward with information they don't realize could help the police find who is behind this."

"But rumors get started and get blown all out of portion, twisted around. It happened years ago when Granddad divorced his first wife. Not long after that he married Winnie. For a while people thought she had taken him away from his first wife, but that wasn't the case. It took years for her to correct those impressions. People had to get to know her to understand she would never come between a man and his wife. It hurt her enough that when I asked her about something I'd heard, she told me what happened."

"I know. I've seen similar cases on the national level, even ones I worked behind the scenes over in the Middle East. The truth often is twisted and blatantly altered."

His hand brushed against her shoulder. "So you see why she's trying to keep all this quiet. Already too many people know about it. I'm afraid she won't be able to. Which brings me to our next problem."

The feel of his fingertips touching her lightly sent her heart racing. His nearness robbed her of coherent thought for a few seconds until she forced herself to concentrate on what he was saying. "I'm afraid to ask what."

"You afraid? All I've seen is a woman cool under pressure."

"There's nothing wrong with being afraid. It keeps me on my toes."

"This Friday night is Glamour Sensations' Christmas Gala. I know my grandmother. Even with what happened tonight, she'll insist on going. She's supposed to introduce Christy as the face of Endless Youth and tease the press with what's going to come in February and the rest of next year."

"I was hoping she would decide not to go and let Harold take care of it."

"My grandmother has always been the spokesperson for the company. Any change will fuel speculation. Glamour Sensations will need the infusion of money by going public if we're to launch and produce the new line the way it should be. If she doesn't show up, some people will think she was badly injured in the wreck."

"Do you think that could be the reason for the wreck? Some competitor wanted to damage what the company is planning to do?"

"Could be." Colt scrubbed his hands down his face. "I wish I knew what was going on. It would make it easier to fight."

"Let me think about what we can do. I certainly don't want to drive to the gala."

"I doubt Winnie would, either, especially with the reminder of Granddad's accident. It took a long while to get over his death. Her heart attack didn't disrupt her life like his dying." He took her hands. "When this is all over with, Harold needs a raise for hiring you. Winnie trusts you. Maybe she'll listen to you about the gala."

"I'll do what I can. Meanwhile I have an idea about how to get her down this mountain without driving."

"How?"

"Use a helicopter. There's plenty of room for it to land in front of the house."

His eyes brightened and he squeezed her hands. "I like that. Winnie should agree, especially given the alternatives."

"I can talk to the sheriff tomorrow to see about who to hire in the area." Then she would have to vet the person in only a few days. But it could be done with her employer's assistance. "If there is no one in the area he'd recommend, we could check Denver or Colorado Springs."

Colt lifted one hand and cupped her face. "You're fantastic."

The gleam in his eyes nearly unraveled her resolve to keep her distance. When this was over with, she would move on to another job and he would return to his research vessel. She needed to remember that. But when his thumb caressed her cheek and he bent toward her, all determination fled in the wake of the soft look in his eyes, as though he saw her as a woman like no other. Special. To be cherished.

His lips whispered across hers before settling over them. He wound one arm around her and brought her close. Her stomach fluttered. Then he enveloped her in an embrace, plastering her against him as he deepened the kiss. Her world tilted. She could taste the coffee on his lips. She could smell his lime-scented aftershave. She could feel the hammering of his heartbeat. Heady sensations overwhelmed her, tempting her to disregard anything logical and totally give in to the feelings he stirred in her.

The realization frightened her more than facing a gunman. She wedged her hands up between them and pushed away from him. The second their mouths parted she missed the feel of his lips on hers. But common sense prevailed. She moved back, putting several feet between them.

"I know I shouldn't have kissed you," Colt said, "but I've wanted to since that first night when you attacked me in the hallway. I've never quite had that kind of homecoming before." One corner of his mouth quirked.

She rose, her legs shaky. "I need to check the house, then go to bed. There's still a lot to do tomorrow."

Before he said or did anything else, she spun on her heel and rushed toward the exit. She considered going outside for some fresh air but decided not to. Instead, she went through the house, making sure the place was secured. Heat blazed her cheeks. She'd wanted the kiss, even wished it could have continued. That would be dangerous, would complicate their situation. But she couldn't get the picture of them kissing out of her mind.

With his hands jammed into his pants' pockets, Colt stood in front of the fireplace in the den and stared at the yellow-orange flames. He'd blown it this evening. He'd had no intention of kissing Ellie, and yet he had. Against his better judgment. What kind of future could they have? He lived on a research vessel in the South Pacific. It wasn't as if he could even carry on a long-distance relationship with a woman. He'd learned from his past attempts at a relationship that he wanted a lasting one like his grandparents had had. Anything less than that wasn't acceptable.

Was that why he'd given up looking for someone? What kind of home could he give her? A berth on a ship? He didn't even call it home. This place on the side of a mountain would always be his home.

He heard her voice coming from the foyer. She said something to the deputy Colt couldn't make out. Peering at the mantel, decorated with garland and gold ribbon for the holidays, he glimpsed the Big Ben clock and the late hour. He needed to go to bed, but he waited until Ellie finished talking with the deputy. He gave her a chance to go upstairs before him because frankly he didn't know what to say to her.

He would have continued the kiss if she hadn't pulled away. His thoughts mocked his declaration to stay away from Ellie St. James, a woman who was fiercely independent and could take care of herself. He'd always wanted someone who would need him. Someone to be an equal partner but rely on him, too.

After taking care of the fire, he moved toward the staircase. Coming home always made him reassess his life. Once he was back on the research vessel he would be fine—back on track with his career and goals.

A few days later Ellie waited for Colt and Winnie in the living room right before they were to leave for Glamour Sensations' Christmas Gala. Dressed in a long black silk gown with a slit up the right side and a gold lamé jacket that came down to the tops of her thighs, she felt uncomfortable. The only place she could put the smaller gun was in a beaded bag she would carry. After all, to the world she was Winnie's assistant, there to make things run smoothly for her employer.

A noise behind her drew her around to watch Colt enter wearing a black tuxedo. She'd only seen him in casual attire. The transformation to a sophisticated gentleman who moved in circles she didn't unless on the job only confirmed how different they were. Yes, he was working on a research ship, but he came from wealth and would inherit a great deal one day. She was from the wrong side of the tracks, a noncommissioned officer in the army for a time and now a woman whose job was to guard others.

He pulled on his cuffs then adjusted his tie. "It's been a while since I wore this. I was all thumbs tying this."

Ellie crossed to him and straightened the bow tie. "There. Perfect."

His smile reached deep into his eyes. "Sometimes I think I need a keeper. I'm much more comfortable in a wet suit or bathing suit."

His remark tore down the barriers she was trying to erect between them. "Tell me about it. I don't like wearing heels. It's hard to run in them."

"Let's hope you don't have to do that tonight."

"I talked with the police chief and his men are in place as well as security from Glamour Sensations. They're checking everyone coming into the ballroom. Thankfully that doesn't seem as out of place as it would have years ago."

She should step away from him, but before she could, he took her hand and backed up a few feet to let his gaze roam leisurely down her length. When it returned to her face, he whistled.

"I like you in heels and that black dress."

She blushed—something she rarely did. "Neither conducive to my kind of work."

"I beg to differ. The bad guy will take one look at you and be so distracted he'll forget what mayhem he was plotting."

Ellie laughed. She would not let his smooth talking go to her head. Two different worlds, she reminded herself. She could see him running Glamour Sensations one day, especially when he told her yesterday he used to work at the company until he finished his college studies.

A loud whirring sound from the front lawn invaded the sudden quiet. She used that distraction to tug her hand free and go to the window. The helicopter landed as close to the house entrance as it could. The dogs barked at it even when the pilot turned it off. Doug Miller called the two Rottweilers back. They obeyed instantly.

"Doug is great with the dogs."

"He was as excited as Granddad when he brought home Rocket and Gabe. Although I don't know if these new ones can ever replace the German shepherds in Doug's and Winnie's hearts. I was hoping we would get a ransom demand or someone would come forward."

"So did I with the nice reward Winnie offered." Ellie rotated from the window and caught sight of the older woman behind her grandson. "You look great, Winnie."

Dignified in a red crepe gown, she walked farther into the room. "I heard the helicopter. Probably our neighbors heard it, too. Never thought of using one to go to a ball."

"It's the modern-day version of Cinderella's coach." Colt offered his arm to his grandmother.

"In that case I fit the Fairy Godmother rather than Cinderella. That role needs to go to you, Ellie."

"Which leaves me as Prince Charming." He winked at Ellie.

Fairy tales were for dreamers, not her. Ellie skirted around the couple and headed for the foyer before she let the talk go to her head. "Well, our version of the story will be altered a tad bit. This Cinderella is taking her Fairy Godmother to the ball and sticking to her side. But I definitely like the idea of us leaving by midnight."

"I may have to go, but I don't have to stay that long."

Ellie stopped and hugged Winnie. "Those were the best words I've heard in a while."

"After dinner I'll make the announcements, stay for questions then leave. We should be home by eleven. I know you aren't happy about me going to the gala, but I owe all the people who have worked years for my company. They'll benefit so much when we go public. A lot of employees will get stock in Glamour Sensations for their loyalty."

Ellie climbed into the helicopter last and searched the area. Where was the person after Winnie? Watching them here? Waiting for Winnie at the hotel or in the ballroom? She clutched her purse, feeling the outline of her gun. Was their security enough?

As employees and guests entered the ballroom, Winnie stood in a greeting line between Colt and Ellie, shaking everyone's hand and taking a moment to talk with each person attending the gala. At first Ellie wasn't thrilled with her client doing that, but it did give her a chance to assess each attendee.

When Christy moved in front of Winnie, her smile grew, and instead of shaking the woman's hand, Winnie enveloped her in a hug. "How was your trip to L.A. for the commercial?"

"A whirlwind. I never knew all that this position would involve. Peter picked me up from the airport late last night, and since I woke up this morning, I've been going nonstop. I'm going to cherish the time we sit down and have dinner tonight."

Winnie took Christy's fiancé's hand and shook it. "It's nice to see you again, Peter. Christy will be in town at least through Christmas. But afterward she'll be busy. I hope you can arrange some time to go with her on some of her trips. I never want to come between two people in love."

Dr. Tyler held Winnie's hand between his for a few extra seconds. "When it's snowing here, I plan on being on that beach when Christy shoots her second commercial next month."

"Perfect solution. I love winter in Colorado, but that beach is beginning to sound good to these old bones."

"Tsk. Tsk. You don't look old at all. It must be your products you use. You should be your own spokesperson."

Colt leaned toward his grandmother. "I've been telling her that for years. She looks twenty years younger than she is. What woman her age wouldn't like to look as youthful?" He gave her a kiss on the cheek.

As Christy and Peter passed Ellie, she said, "You two are seated at the head table. There are place cards where you're to sit."

Peter nodded his head and escorted Christy toward the front of the room, which was decorated in silver and gold. Elegance came to mind as Ellie scanned the spacious area with lights glittering among the rich decor.

Thirty minutes and hundreds of guests later, Winnie greeted the last person. "Every year this event gets bigger."

"This year we have an extra dozen media people here, including our own film crew." Harold took Winnie's arm and started for the head table.

"I guess it's you and me." Colt fell into step next to Ellie, right behind Winnie. "Did you see anyone suspicious?"

"Actually several I'm going to keep an eye on. Did you realize Mary Ann Witlock's brother is here?" Ellie asked, recalling the photo she'd seen in connection with information on Mary Ann Witlock.

"Bob Witlock? He's worked at Glamour Sensations for years."

Winnie paused and turned back. "He's in marketing and agreed that Christy would be better than his younger sister for the position. Before I made the announcement, I talked to him. I wanted him to know first. For that matter, Jerry Olson's daughter works for Glamour Sensations and is here. She's married. I won't hold someone accountable for another's actions, even a close relative."

"Who is Jerry's daughter?" The reports from the sheriff hadn't said anything about that.

"They have been estranged for years, but it's Serena Pitman. She works in the research lab."

If she'd had the time she would have run her own investigation into each of the prime suspects with grudges against Winnie, but she couldn't do everything, which meant she had to rely on information garnered from reliable sources. Sometimes, though, those sources didn't give her everything she might need.

Winnie continued her trek toward the front of the room. Ellie racked her mind with all the guests who had passed before her, trying to remember who Serena Pitman was. Her visual memory was one of her assets. Face after face flitted through her thoughts until she latched onto the one that went with the name Serena

Pitman. Red hair, almost orange, large brown eyes, freckles, petite. She searched the crowd of over two hundred until she found Serena at a table three away from the head one.

When Ellie sat down, her back to the stage, she faced the attendees with a clear view of Serena and her husband. The suspects the police had narrowed down as a viable possibility had not shown up—at least they hadn't come through the greeting line. The security and hotel staff were the only other people besides the guests, and she had made her rounds checking them when she had first arrived before the doors had been opened.

Sandwiched between Winnie and Colt, Ellie assessed each one sitting at the head table. Across from her sat Christy and Peter. Next to the couple was a reporter from the Associated Press and a fashion editor from one of the industry's leading magazines. A Denver newspaper editor of the lifestyle section and a Los Angeles TV show hostess took the last two seats. Harold took his place next to Winnie.

Halfway through the five-course dinner, Colt whispered into Ellie's ear, "Is something wrong with the food?"

"No, it's delicious. I'm not that hungry." Ellie pushed her medley of vegetables around on her plate while her gaze swept over the sea of people, most intent on eating their dinner.

"Everything is going all right."

She slanted a glance at Colt, said, "For the moment," then returned her attention to the crowd.

"Remember, you're Winnie's assistant."

"One who is keeping an eye on the event to make sure it's pulled off without a hitch."

The editor from the Denver newspaper looked right at Winnie and said, "I heard someone earlier talking about a wreck you were involved in. Is that why you arrived here in a helicopter?"

Winnie managed to smile as though nothing was wrong. "A minor collision. It didn't even set off the air bags. A car left stranded in the middle of the highway. Tell me how the drive from Denver was. It was snowing when we arrived."

The man chuckled. "This is Colorado in December. We better have snow or our resort areas will be hurting."

"You're so right, Marvin. Being stranded here isn't too much of a burden. Mountains. Snow. A pair of skis. What more could you ask for?" Winnie cut into her steak.

Harold winked at Winnie. "A warm fire."

"A hot tub," the TV hostess added.

"A snowmobile since I'm probably one of the rare Coloradoans who doesn't ski," Marvin tossed back with the others at the table throwing in other suggestions.

When the conversation started to die down again, Colt asked the Denver editor, "Do you think the Broncos will go all the way to the Super Bowl?"

Ellie bent toward him. "Good question. Football ought to keep the conversation away from the wreck," she whispered.

The mischievous grin on his face riveted her attention for a few long seconds before she averted her gaze and watched the people at the table.

By dessert the conversation morphed from sports to the latest bestsellers. As Peter expounded on a thriller he'd finished, Ellie half listened as she watched the various hotel staff place the peppermint cheesecake before the attendees around the room.

Four tables away Ellie spied a woman who looked vaguely familiar. Was she in one of the photos she'd seen over the past few days? She didn't want to leave Winnie to check the woman out, but she could send a security officer standing not far from her.

"Excuse me, Winnie," Ellie leaned closer to her and whispered, "I'll be right back. I need to talk to your head of security."

Winnie peered over her shoulder at the man

at the bottom of the steps that led to the presentation platform. "A problem?"

"I want him to check someone for me. Probably nothing. Be right back."

"We'll be starting our program in ten minutes. The waiters are serving the dessert and coffee."

The head of Glamour Sensations' security met Ellie halfway. "Is there a problem?"

"The dark-haired woman on the serving staff at the table two from the left wall. She looks familiar. Check her out. See who she is and if she has the proper identification."

He nodded and started in that direction. The woman finished taking a dessert plate from a man, put it on a tray and headed quickly for one of the doors the servers were using. The security chief increased his pace. Ellie slowly walked back toward Winnie, scanning the rest of the room before returning to the woman. The dark-headed lady set the tray on a small table near the door then rushed toward the exit, shoving her way through a couple of waiters. The security chief and a police officer Ellie recognized gave chase.

A couple of guests rose, watching the incident unfold.

Ellie leaned down to Winnie. "You should think about leaving. I think the lady I spotted is who we're after."

Winnie turned her head so no one at the table could see her expression or hear her whisper, "I saw. If she's gone, she can't do anything. I'll start now and run through the program then we can leave."

"Did you recognize her?"

"I couldn't tell from this distance. My eyesight isn't as good as it once was."

"Okay. Then let's get this over with. I'll be right behind you."

Winnie was introducing Christy when the head of security came back into the ballroom. He shook his head and took up his post at the foot of the steps to the platform. Ellie noted that all the doors were covered so the woman couldn't return to disrupt the presentation.

Christy came up to stand by Winnie, their arms linked around each other as they faced the audience clapping and cheering. Behind the pair, the screen showed some of the Endless Youth products being released in February. At the height of the event the confetti guns shot off their loads to fill the room with red-and-green streamers. A festival atmosphere took hold of the crowd.

Through the celebration Ellie hovered near Winnie, fixing her full attention on the crowd. Not long and they would all be back in the helicopter returning to the estate. She would be glad when that happened.

Some colorful streamers landed near Ellie, followed by a glass vial that shattered when it hit the platform. A stinking smell wafted up to her. Coughing, Ellie immediately rushed to Winnie's side as more vials mixed in with the streamers smashed against the floor through-out the ballroom, saturating the place with an awful, nauseating stench. People panicked and fled for the doors. The gaiety evolved into pandemonium almost instantly.

Chapter Eight

Over the screams and shouts, Colt hopped up onto the platform and reached Winnie's side just as Ellie tugged her toward the steps.

"We need to get out of here," she told them. "This would be a great time to strike in the midst of this chaos."

Colt wound his arm about his grandmother. Winnie faltered at the bottom of the stairs. He caught her at the same time Ellie turned and grabbed her, too. Their gazes met.

"We can get out this way." Ellie nodded toward a door behind the staging area. "It leads to an exit. All we have to do is get to the helicopter."

"But the announcement and celebration are ruined," Winnie mumbled, glancing back once before being ushered through the door and down a long hall.

His grandmother looked as if she were shell-shocked. He couldn't blame her. He, too, had hoped they could make it through the evening without incident.

"Once I get you home, I'll check to see what happened. Knowing the police chief and the sheriff, they are already on it." Ellie removed her gun from her purse.

The sight of the lethal weapon widened his grandmother's eyes at the same time the color drained from her face. He tightened his arms about her. She was a remarkable woman, but anyone could hit a wall and fall apart. He was afraid she was there.

At the door that led outside, Ellie held up her hand to stop them. "Wait. Let me check the area out." She searched the long hallway. "Be right back."

He looked over his shoulder at a few people rushing down the corridor toward the exit.

A couple of seconds later, Ellie returned. "Let's go. The helicopter is around the corner. People are pouring out of the hotel, but it's clear on this side."

"Not for long." Colt tossed his head toward the people coming down the hall.

With her hand on Winnie's right arm, Ellie led the way. She'd seen the pilot in the chopper and his instructions earlier were to start the engine the second he saw them approaching. Colt flanked his grandmother on the left and slightly behind her as though shielding her from anyone behind. Ellie did this as a job. He did it because he loved his grandmother enough to protect her with his life.

As she neared the front lawn of the hotel, Ellie slowed, panning the terrain for any sign of someone lying in wait. The woman who could have been behind what occurred in the ballroom might have planned the chaos so she could get to Winnie easier outside in the open. Ellie wouldn't allow that to happen.

Peering around the corner of the hotel, Ellie scoped out the crowd emerging from the front entrance, many with no coats on, who stood hugging themselves. The biting cold penetrated the thin layer of her lamé jacket. The people behind them in the hallway burst from the exit, their loud voices charged with fear and speculation.

"Let's go." Ellie started across the snow-covered ground.

A man hurried toward the helicopter as the blades began to whir.

Her gaze glued to the exchange between the pilot and the stranger, Ellie shortened her strides, waiting to see what transpired. When the man ran back toward the crowd, she increased her speed again. The sound of sirens blasted the chilly air.

At the chopper Colt assisted Winnie up into it while Ellie kept watch on the surroundings. After Colt followed his grandmother into the helicopter, Ellie climbed in and the pilot lifted off.

Over the whirring noise, Ellie spoke into her headset. "Who was that man?"

"Hotel security letting me know what happened in the ballroom. I figured you'd be outside soon." The pilot made a wide arc and headed toward the estate.

Ten minutes more. Ellie didn't let down her guard. Sitting forward, she scanned the terrain below. A blanket of white carpeted the ground, lighting the landscape. A helicopter ride she'd taken during one of her missions in the army flashed into her mind. Insurgents on the ground had fired on it, wounding one person in the backseat.

"Winnie, move as far over toward Colt as you can."

As her client did, Colt wrapped his arms around her. Again trying to shield her as much as he could.

Nine minutes later the pilot brought the chopper down as close to the main house as possible. Ellie scrambled out and hurried to Winnie's side to help her. The second she placed her feet on the drive, Ellie shepherded the woman toward her front door while the dogs barked at the helicopter.

Colt gave a command, and they quieted. He came up behind Ellie as they mounted the steps to the deck. Doug threw open the front door, and Ellie whisked Winnie inside.

"The sheriff called and said he's on his way," the caretaker said. "He briefly told me what happened so I came over. I figured you'd be back soon."

Through the fear that marked Winnie's face, she smiled. "I can always count on you and Linda."

"She's in the kitchen preparing some coffee. She'll bring it into the den. I'll let the sheriff in when he's at the gate."

On the way to the den, Ellie paused in the doorway of the small control room. "Have you seen anything unusual?" she asked the ex-police chief who monitored the security feed.

"Nope. Quiet."

Ellie caught up with Winnie and Colt as they entered the den. While Ellie walked from window to window, drawing the drapes, her client collapsed onto the couch, sagging back, her eyes sliding closed.

"Winnie, are you all right?" Colt sat beside her.

"No. This has got to stop. Everything was ruined tonight. Poor Christy. This was her big debut, and some mean, vicious person destroyed her moment."

Ellie positioned herself in front of the fireplace close to Winnie but facing the only entrance into the room. She still clutched her gun as though it were welded to her hand.

"I want to thank you for getting me out of there, Ellie. I'd still be standing on stage, stunned by the lengths a person will go to hurt another."

Ellie moved to the couch and sat on the other side of Winnie. Not until she took a seat did she relax her tightly bunched muscles. "I was only doing my job."

"You've done much more than that for me. The Lord sent you to me at this time." Winnie patted Colt's leg. "And you were there for me, too. I have truly been blessed having two people like you seeing to my welfare." Tears shone in her eyes.

Ellie thanked her. "I got a look at someone I suspect may be the one causing the trouble. Hopefully this might be over before Christmas. I'm still not sure from where I know that woman at the gala tonight, but when security approached, she ran. That's not the action of an innocent person." The sound of footsteps returned Ellie's attention to the door, her hand tensing again on her gun.

Linda entered with a tray of four mugs and a coffeepot. "Doug let the sheriff in the front gate. He should be here any minute. After he arrives, we'll leave unless you need me for anything, Winnie."

She shook her head, a few strands escaping her usual neatly styled silver-gray bun at her nape. "You two are up late as it is. I'm glad you didn't go to the Christmas Gala. Not after what happened."

"Doug and I felt we needed to stay here and make sure nothing went wrong from this end. He patrolled the grounds with the dogs. You know how he is when it starts snowing. He'd rather be outside than in the house." Linda placed the tray on the table in front of the couch. "Do you want me to pour the coffee?"

Colt scooted forward. "I'll do it. Tell Doug thanks."

Doug appeared in the entrance with the sheriff. Linda crossed to them and left with her husband.

Sheriff Quinn grabbed the mug Colt held out to him. "It's getting cold outside."

Winnie didn't hesitate to ask her questions. "Bill, what happened? Is everyone all right? I'm assuming since I don't feel sick that what was released into the air wasn't poisonous."

"You're right, Winnie. Thankfully they were only stink bombs. The police are still trying to determine how many. There were five confetti guns, and it looks like each one shot at least one vial out of it. Maybe more."

"Any injuries with the stampede for the doors?" Ellie cradled her hot mug between her palms. She'd been caught up in a riot once and knew how easily people could get hurt when everyone was trying to flee a place.

"Right before I arrived, the police chief called to let me know he has access to the security feed at the hotel. He said so far it looks like ten injuries, mostly minor stuff. One woman is being sent to the hospital, but I don't think she will stay long."

"It could have been a lot worse." The firm line of Colt's jaw and the extra-precise way he set his mug down attested to his tightly controlled anger.

The sheriff looked at Ellie. "The police chief wants you to look at the tapes of the event. He understands from Glamour Sensations' security head that you think you recognized someone who fled out the staff door. We need to ID that person."

"Sure. I'll do anything I can, but I don't want to leave the estate. Not when Winnie is in danger."

"I thought you would say that. We'll have access to the tapes by computer. It'll be a good time for you all to look over the footage and see if anyone is out of place."

"Anything, even watching hours of tape," Colt said. "I want this to end. My grandmother has been through enough. All I can say is that I'm glad her last product development has been concluded."

"Hon, I'm fine, especially with you and Ellie here." She patted Colt's hand. "Dear, get my laptop from my lab downstairs, will you please?"

Right before he disappeared down the hall, Colt threw a look at Ellie while Winnie and the sheriff talked. In that moment Ellie saw how worried Colt was for his grandmother. Again, she found herself wishing she had that bond with someone.

Sheriff Quinn interrupted her thoughts. "The police are rounding up the staff to question them. If we could have a picture to show them, that will help."

Ellie closed her eyes and imagined the woman from across the ballroom. "She's about five feet six inches with long dark hair. I couldn't tell her eye color specifically, but I think a light color.

She was dressed as a server—even had a name tag on like the others."

"I'll let the police chief know that. See if anyone is missing a uniform. If not, it could be one of their staff even if the person wasn't supposed to work that event. Did you see who Ellie is talking about?" he asked Winnie.

"No, sorry. I was trying to keep the conversation at the table going in the right direction. As I suspected, a few rumors have been flying around. The AP reporter wanted confirmation the position of the stolen car indicated it was probably left deliberately, possibly to block our way home."

"Sheriff, did you find any fingerprints on the stalled car the other night?" Ellie leaned over, refilled her mug and poured some more coffee into Winnie's.

"The report came in. No fingerprints the owner couldn't verify weren't someone's who has been in the car lately. So no help there."

Colt came back into the den and handed the laptop to the sheriff to pull up the site with the security footage on it. When he had it, he turned it around and set it on the coffee table, then walked behind the couch to watch.

Sheriff Quinn pointed to a link. "Click on that."

Colt did and a scene from inside the ballroom popped up on the screen. They watched that angle, but Ellie couldn't find the woman or anyone else that appeared suspicious. Colt went to the next link and brought it up.

Ten minutes into it, Winnie yawned. "I'm sorry. I don't know if I can stay awake."

As her own adrenaline rush had subsided, obviously Winnie's had, too. Ellie was used to the ups and downs, but her client wasn't. "Sheriff, can she review it tomorrow morning? I may want to see them again, too."

"Sure." He turned to Winnie. "I can escort you to your room."

Colt paused the tape while Winnie struggled to her feet, sighed and stepped around her grandson. "No, you should stay. At least this person hasn't come into my home and threatened me. If I couldn't walk freely in my own house, I don't know what I would do."

When Winnie left, Ellie murmured, "I didn't have the heart to tell her there is no place one hundred percent secure."

Colt scooted over so the sheriff could sit on the couch. "You don't think it's safe here?"

"Basically it is, as much as it can be. Or I wouldn't let Winnie walk around by herself without me right there. But in any situation I've learned to be wary."

"On the research vessel we've had two run-ins with pirates in different locales, which keeps us on the watch wherever we go, but nothing like this." Colt clicked to continue viewing the security footage.

"It's sad," Ellie said, focusing again on the tape. "These kinds of things are what keep me in business."

"Pause it. That's her!" About an hour into the footage Ellie bolted forward, pointing at a dark-haired woman on the screen who was carrying a tray with coffeepots and a water pitcher. "The same height, hairstyle. Can we zoom in on her?"

Colt clicked several keys and moved in closer.

"That's who ran out of the ballroom when the security head made his way toward her. We need a still of that, and see if someone can make the photo clearer." Her image teased Ellie's thoughts.

"I'll see what I can do and bring it back to you tomorrow." Sheriff Quinn wrote down how far into that tape they were while Colt started the footage again.

On closer examination, Ellie saw surprise on the woman's face when she spied the two security men coming toward her. She glanced toward a table near the head table, then hurried toward the exit. "Back up. Who was she looking at?"

Colt found the spot and zeroed in on the table next to the one where they'd been sitting. "Take your pick who she's staring at."

"Maybe no one." The sheriff rose.

"Or maybe one of the people whose back isn't to the woman," Ellie said. "There are four men and three women. Is there any way we can find out who was sitting at the table? There were only a few tables reserved and that wasn't one of them."

"I'll see what I can find out tomorrow morning when I meet with the police chief. In the meantime, I'm leaving two deputies with you again. One is in the foyer. The other is driving up the mountain as we speak. Rod will let him in. We'll have a long day tomorrow so get some sleep. That's what I'm gonna do. I'm determined we'll find out who it is. We have a picture now. That's better than before."

"Sheriff, I love your optimism. I hope you're right. I could be home in time for Christmas." She walked with him out to the foyer where Rod stood.

"Where is home?"

"Dallas, when I'm between jobs."

"Family there?"

"No. It'll just be me, but my boss hosts Christmas dinner for anyone who's in town." Which was the closest she came to having a family during the holidays.

"I have a son coming in for Christmas with his three children. I can't wait to see them. It's been six months, and they grow up fast."

When Ellie returned to the den, Colt gathered up the closed laptop and bridged the distance between them. "I heard what you said about Christmas. Do you think this will be over by then? That we'll have a peaceful Christmas?"

"I'm hoping. Winnie has been great dealing with what's been happening to her, but it's taking its toll."

"I'm glad she's finished in the lab. She doesn't have to worry about that at least."

"But that will mean she'll focus totally on what's happening. That may be worse."

"Then we'll have to create things for her to do. We haven't decorated the house like it has been in the past. Tons of decorations are still in storage in the basement."

Ellie couldn't remember decorating for Christmas in years, and even as a child, they often didn't have a tree. Her mother didn't care about the holiday, but Toby and she had tried to make their apartment festive. Then Toby had died and Ellie hadn't cared, either. "Sure, if it will help take Winnie's mind off the threats."

"Christmas is her favorite time of year. She's

been so busy she's not had the time to do what she usually does. This will be perfect." Colt strode to the staircase with Ellie.

As she mounted the steps to the second floor, she wondered what a family Christmas was really like. At the top of the stairs, she looked around and started laughing. "I can't believe I walked all the way up here when I haven't checked the house yet."

"It must have been my charm and wit that rattled you."

"I hate to burst your bubble, Colt, but it's exhaustion." The sound of his chuckles sent a wave of warmth down her length.

"I'll put this laptop in my room and come with you. I wouldn't want you to fall asleep while making your rounds." He turned toward the right.

Ellie clasped his arm. "I'll be okay. I may be exhausted, but that doesn't mean I'll fall asleep."

He swung around. His gaze intent, he grazed his fingertips down her jaw. "What keeps you from sleeping?"

She shrugged one shoulder. "The usual. Worries."

"Winnie would tell you to turn them over to the Lord."

"What would you say?"

"Winnie is right, but I've always had trouble doing that. I still want to control things."

"Me, too. I know worrying is a waste of time and energy, but I've been doing it for so long, trying to control all aspects of my life, that I don't know how to give it totally to God."

"Practice."

"Have you ever practiced and practiced and never accomplished what you set out to do?"

"Not usually." He snapped his finger. "Except ballroom dancing. I have two left feet."

"I'll remember that if you ever ask me to dance." She took a step back. "Seriously, you don't need to come with me. At least one of us should get some sleep. I'm not going to bed until the second deputy arrives, anyway."

"I can keep you company if you like."

She would, but as she stared into his face, a face she'd looked forward to seeing each morning, she knew the danger in him staying up with her. Each day she was around him she liked him more and more. The way he loved his grandmother, handled a crisis—the way he kissed. "No, I'm not going to be long." She backed up until her heel encountered the edge of the staircase.

Like the first night they met, he moved with a quickness that surprised her, hooked his arm around her and tugged her to him. He planted a kiss on her lips that melted her resolve not to be around him. Then he parted, pivoted and started down the hallway. "Good night, Ellie. I'll see you in the morning."

Why did you do that? She wanted to shout the question at him but clamped together her tingling lips that still felt the remnants of his kiss. Coupled with her stomach fluttering and her heart beating rapidly, the sensations from that brief joining left their brand on her. She hurried down the stairs, sure the only reason she was attracted to the man was because it was that time of year when she yearned for a family, for a connectedness she'd never had except with her twin brother, Toby.

As Ellie went from room to room, making sure the house was secured, she forced her mind back to the case. She visualized the picture of the woman on the computer in her mind. She'd seen her before. By the time she reached her bedroom, she strode to the photos the sheriff had shown them of the possible suspects. She flipped through the pictures until she came upon Mary Ann Witlock. Covering up the woman's long blond hair, Ellie visualized her in a dark brown wig. And that's when she knew. Mary Ann was the bogus server at the gala tonight.

* * *

"Hot chocolate for everyone," Linda announced the next afternoon as she brought in a tray with the drinks and a plate of frosted Christmas sugar cookies.

For the past couple hours Ellie had been decorating a tree with Colt and Winnie and Harold and Christy. Now she climbed the ladder to place the star at the very top. When she descended to the floor, she viewed the ten-foot tree Doug and Colt had cut down that morning. The scent of pine hung in the air.

"This is turning into a party. I love it." Winnie backed away from the tree in the living room centered in front of the large picture window. "I might not be able to leave, but I appreciate you all coming here to help cheer up an old lady. This is just what I needed."

Colt slung his arm over his grandmother's shoulders. "Old? Did I hear you admit you're old? Who has stolen my grandmother?"

Winnie punched him playfully in the stomach. "I am seventy-three."

Colt arched a eyebrow. "So?"

"Okay, I admit I've let the threats get to me. But not anymore. The sheriff is closing in on the woman who, it looks like, has been behind everything."

"I can't believe Mary Ann is behind this. If

I'd known what would happen, I'd have turned down the opportunity to be the spokesperson for Endless Youth." Christy took a mug of hot chocolate and a cookie off the tray. "I didn't realize she needed the money."

Winnie frowned. "Neither did I. If she had come to me, I would have loaned her the money."

"We don't know for sure it's her behind the threats," Harold said as he planted himself in a chair. "All we know is she was disguised last night as a server and then ran from security when approached."

"That's the action of a guilty person. And why was she wearing a dark wig if she was innocent?" Linda asked as she left the room.

"What do you think, Ellie?" Winnie removed some tinsel from a box and passed it out.

"She needs money and lost a chance at making a lot. She is missing right now. The police went to her house and haven't been able to locate her. Maybe the search warrant will produce something more concrete." Ellie carefully draped a few strands of tinsel on a branch. Probably the person Mary Ann was looking at before fleeing the ballroom was her brother, sitting at the table next to them. When Winnie had identified him this morning on the video, that was at least one mystery taken care of. Sheriff Quinn was investigating Bob Witlock to make sure he had no involvement, but he didn't think the brother did because he and Mary Ann had been estranged for several years.

Colt came up beside Ellie. "At the rate you're going, Ellie, it'll be midnight before we finish decorating the tree. This is the way we do it." He took some of the tinsel and tossed it onto several limbs. "See? Effective and fast."

"But it's not neat."

"That's okay. It's fun, and our tree isn't what you would find in a magazine. It's full of our past—not fancy store-bought ornaments." Colt gave her some more tinsel. "Give it a try."

Ellie did and laughed when half ended up on the carpet. "There must be an art to it, and clearly I don't have the toss method down."

Colt stepped behind her and took her arm. "It's called losing a little control and just letting go at the right time," he whispered into her ear.

She was glad no one else could hear him; his words caused her pulse rate to accelerate.

As he brought her arm back then swung it forward, he murmured, "Let go."

In the second she did and the silvery strands landed on various branches haphazardly, but none on the floor, something inside her did let go. It had nothing to do with the activity. It had to do with the man so close to her his scent engulfed her. The brush of his breath against her neck warmed her.

Quickly she stepped away. "I have no idea when I'll use this new skill again, but thanks for showing me how to do it properly." She tore her gaze from his and swept it around the room, taking in the faces of the people, all of whom were watching them.

The chime of the doorbell cut through the silence that fell over the room. Ellie thrust the remaining tinsel into Colt's hands and hurried to answer the door. She'd let him get to her. Let him give her a little glimpse at what she was missing. And she became all soft.

She opened the door to allow the sheriff inside. "I hope you have good news for us. What did you find at Mary Ann's house?"

He faced her with a grim expression. "We found a lot of evidence that points to her being the person threatening Winnie—one letter Winnie received was on Mary Ann's computer, along with pictures of Winnie. There was also a suicide note from Mary Ann. When I turned the computer on, that was the first thing that came up."

"Suicide? You found her body?"

"No. No one has seen her since last night. The Bakersville police and my office are still searching for her. There were also a couple of large dog crates in her garage and mud-caked boots, size nine men's shoes, although that isn't the size she wears. Also, there was a stack of unpaid bills on her kitchen table. She received a foreclosure notice a week ago."

"Winnie won't be safe until Mary Ann is found. I hope alive. But what about the dogs? If she took them, where are they?" Out of the corner of her eye she glimpsed Colt coming across the foyer toward them.

"Good question," the sheriff replied. "She could have gotten rid of them or sold them perhaps to someone not from around here. She needed money, so that would be my guess."

"So there's no telling where the dogs are, then?"

Colt stopped next to her. "Winnie was concerned something has happened."

"It has. It looks like Mary Ann is the person threatening Winnie, but she's disappeared." Ellie tried not to look at Colt directly in the eyes. Something had changed between them earlier in the living room, and she didn't know what to think or what to do about it.

"Which means Winnie is still in danger."

"Afraid so," the sheriff said, removing his hat and sliding the brim through his hands.

Winnie paused in the doorway into the living room. "Bill, why are you all standing out here?

Come join us. Harold is here and Christy. Peter is coming after his last patient. We're getting ready for Christmas finally."

"I hate to intrude—"

"We've got hot chocolate and Christmas cookies."

"Well, in that case, I'll stay for a little while." The sheriff made his way toward Winnie, grinning from ear to ear. "Linda makes great cookies. I bought a box of them at the cookie sale at church."

"Why, Bill Quinn, I could have made them."

Both of his eyebrows rose. "Did you?"

Winnie giggled. "No, you're safe from my cooking. Why do you think I hired Linda in the first place?"

"Your husband insisted."

As the two entered the living room and their voices faded, Ellie hung back with Colt. "I wanted to let you know what the sheriff told me when they went to Mary Ann's house." After she explained what they found, she added, "There was a suicide note on her computer."

"But she wasn't there?"

"No. The woman isn't in her right mind. She's desperate. What she did last night is an act of a person falling apart. An act of revenge."

"And the dogs? Any idea where they are?"

"They're valuable dogs. No telling where they

are now. She most likely sold them since she was in debt for thousands of dollars. The police chief is checking with the bank in Bakersville where Mary Ann had an account to see if she was paid a large amount of money lately."

"If that's the case, couldn't she take care of some of her debt, if not all?"

"I did some research on some of the suspects, and I remember she had extensive dental work six months ago. I saw a before and after picture. Her teeth and smile were perfect afterward. It made a big difference in her appearance. I wonder if she did that hoping she would get the spokesperson position for Endless Youth."

"If that were the case, I can see why Winnie wouldn't hire her. She wouldn't want anyone who'd recently had work done to her face, even dental. The press could take it and focus on that rather than on Endless Youth. I've seen it before. Where the intended message is sidetracked by something that really had nothing to do with it."

"She had a huge dental bill and her waitress salary probably barely covered her necessities."

Winnie appeared in the living room entrance and peered at Colt. "We have guests. You two can talk after they leave. I imagine you're speculating about Mary Ann, and I would like to hear what you have to say. She needs our prayers, the troubled girl."

"Sorry, Winnie," Colt replied. "We didn't want to say anything in front of the others."

"It's only Christy and Harold. They're family. Oh, that reminds me. I've got to let the person monitoring the gate know to let Peter in when he arrives. I thought we'd have an early dinner before sending our guests down the mountain. And the sheriff is staying, too. It seems his office can run without him occasionally." Winnie hurried toward the monitoring room.

"Are you sure she is really seventy-three?" Ellie asked as she headed for the living room.

"That's what her birth certificate said. I saw it once before she whisked it away from me. That was when she wouldn't tell anyone her age."

"She should be the spokesperson for Endless Youth."

"You know Harold mentioned that to her, and she laughed in his face. I could never see my grandmother purposely putting herself in the public eye."

"Because of what happened when she married your grandfather?"

"Partly, and the fact that Winnie is really shy with most people."

"Shy? I don't see much evidence of that. Look at last night with the media before everything fell apart."

"She's learned to put on a front and can do

it for short periods of time, but, believe me, the evening drained her emotionally beyond the threats and what happened with the stink bombs."

"No wonder I like her so much. She and I have a lot in common."

"I know. That's why I like you."

His words took flight in her heart until she shot them down. They didn't mean anything. Really.

Soft strains of Christmas music played in the background. The fire blazed in the hearth in the living room while the hundreds of lights strung around the tree and a lone lamp gave off the only illumination. Colt settled on the couch next to Winnie, with Harold at the other end. Ellie sat directly across from him. Cuddling as two people in love did, Christy and Peter shared an oversize lounge chair. Sheriff Quinn had left hours ago.

Cozy. Warm. Almost as if there had been no threats, no attempts on Winnie. Almost. But the thought had edged its way into Colt's mind throughout the day, souring a day meant to forget the incident at the gala and to focus on Christmas. Then he would look at Ellie and the outside world wouldn't mean anything.

Doug came into the room. "Before Linda and

I leave, I thought I'd let you know that it has started snowing again. We're not supposed to get too much."

"Thank Linda for another wonderful dinner." Winnie set her coffee on a coaster on the table.

"We enjoyed sharing the celebration tonight with all of you, but I want to check on the dogs," Doug said. "We both hope they find this Mary Ann Witlock soon so this is all over with." After saying his goodbyes the caretaker left.

Colt had always felt his grandmother was in good hands with the couple who had become more a part of the family with each year. "I wish the sheriff would call us with some good news. Maybe Mary Ann fled the area."

"Sheriff Quinn said they checked the airports in the vicinity, but Mary Ann's car is gone so she might have. They have a multistate search out for the car." Ellie leaned back and crossed her long legs.

The movement drew Colt's attention, his eyes slowly making their way up her body to her face. The soft glow of the lighting in the room emphasized her beauty. What was it about Ellie that intrigued him? That she could take care of herself in just about any situation? He knew strong women, even worked with several on the research vessel, but other than respecting their intelligence, there was no draw for him—not like with Ellie.

"We all know there are plenty of places to hide in the mountains around here. Back roads to use." Peter shifted then circled his arm around Christy.

"Yeah, but it's winter and snow will make that more difficult," Harold said.

Peter came right back with, "We haven't had as much as usual so far this year. She may be long gone by now."

"True. And when you're desperate, you sometimes do things you wouldn't normally do." Ellie's gaze fixed on Colt as though there was a secret message behind her words.

"I know she was at Glamour Sensations a lot for the Endless Youth position, but she was always so quiet and reserved. I didn't really know her at all." Christy peered over her shoulder at Peter. "You did her dental work. Didn't you see her for a follow-up a few weeks ago? What do you think her frame of mind was like?"

"She was agitated. She asked me to extend the time she could pay off her bill. I did, but she still was upset when she left. If I'd thought she would commit suicide, I'd have said something, but…"

"Peter, we can't always tell what someone is thinking or is going to do. I know we all would have said something if we had known. I'm still praying the police will find her alive and hiding." Winnie's hand quivered as she brought her cup to her lips.

Colt slid his arm around his grandmother. "You'd be the first one to help her if you'd known. If she's found, I wouldn't be surprised if you pay for a good lawyer to defend her. That's one of the things I love about you."

A frown puckered Christy's forehead. "Can we change the subject? I don't want to spend any more time on this horrid situation. I feel bad enough about Mary Ann."

Winnie patted Colt's thigh, then smiled at Christy. "You're right. Let's talk about our plans for Christmas. Only three days away."

Ellie's cell rang. She looked at the number then rose, leaving the room. Colt heard her say Sheriff Quinn's name and followed her into the foyer.

As he neared her, she ended the call and lifted her gaze to his. "They found Mary Ann's body."

Chapter Nine

Ellie slipped her cell into her pocket. "Her body was found at the bottom of a cliff by cross-country skiers right before dark. Her car, parked near the top of the cliff, was found by a deputy a little later."

"Suicide?"

"That's what they think, but Sheriff Quinn will know more tomorrow after the medical examiner looks at the body and they have more time to thoroughly search the scene below and above. The preliminary processing supports a suicide, especially in light of her note and state of mind."

Colt blew out a long breath. "Then it's over with."

"It's looking that way."

"Let's go tell everyone." Colt held his hand out to her.

She took it, realizing by tomorrow or the following day she could be on her way back to Dallas. Just in time to spend a lonely Christmas at home. At least she'd have a few hours with Kyra and her husband on the twenty-fifth.

When they reentered the living room Colt sat next to Winnie. "Ellie heard from the sheriff. They found Mary Ann's body at the bottom of a cliff. They think it was suicide but they'll make a ruling probably tomorrow."

"It's over. That's great." Standing at the fireplace, Harold dropped another log on the blaze. "The best news I've heard in a while."

"Harold! How can you say that? A young woman killed herself." Tears glittered on Winnie's bottom eyelashes.

The CFO flushed, redder than the flames behind him. "You're right. I was only thinking about you and your situation."

"She did try to kill you." Peter sat forward. "There are people last night who were hurt because of her rage. *You* could have been hurt in the stampede to leave. Or when you were outside. Surely the stink bombs were a ruse to get you outside."

Winnie pushed to her feet. "I don't care. I can't celebrate a woman's death."

Colt stood up beside her. "Grandma, I don't

think Harold really meant that. He was just showing how happy he is that it's all over."

Harold crossed to Winnie and took her into his arms. "I'm sorry. I never meant to cause you any pain. Please forgive me."

She raised her chin and looked at him. "I know you didn't. I only wish I'd known what was going on in Mary Ann's head. I could have helped her."

Could she forgive like that? Ellie wondered. She still couldn't forgive her mother for her neglect as she and Toby grew up. If Toby hadn't had Ellie, he would have had no one to look out for him. He'd needed extra care, and their mother couldn't be bothered.

"I applaud you for wanting to help the woman, but she did try to hurt you." Peter shook his head slowly. "Aren't you just a little bit angry at her? That's a natural human response to someone who does something to you."

Winnie withdrew from Harold's embrace. "Did I ever feel anger toward the person behind the threats? Of course, I did. I'm no saint. But if I let that anger take over, I'm the one who is really hurt by it."

Peter snorted. "You're really hurt if they succeed in their plan. I'm sorry. I think people should be held accountable for what they do."

"I have to agree with Peter," Colt said. "Mary

Ann had choices. I can't make excuses for what she put you through. I certainly won't celebrate her death, but I'm relieved it's over with. We can all have a normal Christmas." He looked from Winnie to Ellie.

Silence hovered over the group as his gaze drew her to him. Ellie gripped the back of a chair and remained still, finally averting her eyes.

"We'd better head home. I don't want to get caught out in a snowstorm." Peter rose right after Christy and put his arm around his fiancée. "Our time is limited since Christy found out she needed to go back to L.A. for a couple of days."

"Since when?" Winnie asked.

"Since last night." Harold kneaded her shoulder. "I forgot to tell you. I meant to first thing this afternoon, then we started decorating the tree. She is going to appear on *Starr's Take*. The talk show hostess felt bad about what happened last night and wants to highlight Christy for a show at the first of the year. That is, if Christy will fly to L.A. tomorrow and tape the segment first thing the next day."

"I'll be back midafternoon Christmas Eve. I don't want to miss my first one with Peter." Christy clasped his hand. "We had plans, but he's been so good about it."

"Harold, I can't believe you didn't tell me the second you walked into my house," Winnie said.

"If you remember correctly, you dragged me over to the box of lights and told me to untangle them."

Winnie's eyes twinkled. "Oh, that's right. In that case, I know what it's like to be distracted. I've had my share of distractions these past few weeks. No more. I'm diving into Christmas. I might even persuade my grandson to go up to my cabin like we used to."

"Not unless the sheriff approves, Winnie." Harold gave her a kiss on the cheek and prepared to leave.

Winnie walked with Harold, Peter and Christy to the foyer while Colt stayed back, snatching Ellie as she started to follow his grandmother. "I can't believe this may be over."

"If it is tomorrow, when are you going back to your research vessel?"

"I'm definitely staying through Christmas now. I want to make sure Winnie is all right. She can beat herself up when she finds out someone is hurting and she didn't do anything about it. I don't want her to start blaming herself for not anticipating Mary Ann's reaction to not getting the job with Endless Youth."

"We can't control other people's reactions, only our own."

Winnie strode into the room. "You two don't have to worry about me. I'm going to be fine, especially if I can spend some time at the cabin like we used to every Christmas."

"So you really are thinking about going up the mountain?" Colt asked.

"Yes, I know we spent the day decorating the house, but all of this has made me yearn for those simpler days. Thomas and I loved to escape life by going to the cabin."

"My fondest memories are of our Christmases spent there."

"So you'll agree to go?" Winnie picked up the coffee cups and put them on the tray Doug had left earlier.

"Yes."

Winnie looked up from the coffee table. "How about you, Ellie? I'd love for you to join us. You're part of the reason I'm safe and able to go to the cabin. It would be nice to share it with you."

"I hate to intrude—"

"Nonsense. I remember you saying that you don't have family to spend the holidays with. Consider us your family this year." Winnie started to lift the tray.

Colt hurried forward and took it from her. "I

agree with Winnie. After all the time you've spent protecting her, let us show our appreciation. Please."

The look he gave Ellie warmed her insides. She wasn't quite ready yet to say goodbye to him or Winnie. Which, if she thought about it, was probably a mistake. Clearly she had feelings for them—and she didn't do emotions well. Still, maybe it was time just to do something impulsive. "I'll join you, if you're sure."

"Well, then it's settled. We'll go if the sheriff thinks it's okay." Winnie walked toward the hallway. "I'm suddenly tired. It's been quite a day—actually, quite a week."

After she left to retire for the night, Colt's gaze seized Ellie's, a smoldering glint in his gray-blue eyes. "What about you?"

"I'm surprised I'm not tired. Maybe I had one too many cups of coffee. Caffeine usually doesn't affect me, though."

"I'll be right back. I'm known around the *Kaleidoscope* as the night owl, the last to go to sleep and definitely not the first to wake up in the morning."

As Colt left with the tray, the warmth of the fire drew Ellie to the sofa nearest the fireplace. She decided that for a short time she was going to enjoy herself. Real life would return when she flew back to Dallas and took another assignment.

Settling herself on the couch, she lounged back, resting her head against the cushion. The faint sounds of "Silent Night" played in the background. She remembered a Christmas Eve service she went to years ago where at the end the lights were switched off and only candlelight glowed in the dark church. She reached over and shut off the lamp nearby, throwing the room in shadows with only the tree and fire for illumination.

With a sigh, she relaxed, though she knew she couldn't surrender her guard totally. Nothing was official concerning Mary Ann. The sheriff still had a few loose ends he wanted cleared up.

She heard Colt move across the room toward her. The air vibrated with his presence although he was quiet. The cushion gave in when he sat on the sofa only inches from her. His scent vied with the aromas of the fire and the pine tree.

"Ellie," he whispered as though he might wake her up if he spoke any louder.

"I can't fall asleep that fast." She opened her eyes and rolled her head to the side to look at him. "I was enjoying the sound of the music and the crackling of the fire."

"I can always leave you—"

She touched her fingertips to his lips. "Shh.

The sound of your voice is even better. Tell me about what it was like growing up with Winnie. What happened to your parents?"

He leaned back, his arm up against hers. "I never really knew my mother. She died shortly after I was born. A massive infection. I guess my father tried to raise me—or more like a series of nannies did. One day when I was four Winnie showed up at the house and found the nanny drinking my dad's liquor. Winnie took me home with her, and I never left after that."

"What about your father?"

"I saw him occasionally when he wanted something from his parents. Mostly I just heard about his exploits from the servants or sometimes from the news. He played fast and furious. Never cared about the family business. One day he mixed drugs and alcohol, passed out and never woke up. Winnie told me he was mourning my mother's death. According to my grandmother, he loved her very much and fell apart when she died."

"How do you feel about your dad?"

Colt tensed, sitting up. "I hardly knew the man, so how can I answer that?"

"Truthfully. You might not have known him well, but that doesn't stop you from forming an opinion, having feelings about him."

For a long moment he sat quietly, his hands

clasped together tightly, staring at the coffee table. "The truth is I don't have much feeling toward him at all. He was the man who happened to sire me, but he wasn't my father. My granddad filled that position in my life. The same with Winnie. She was my mother."

"Do you blame your mother for dying?"

He turned toward her, again not saying anything, but a war of emotions flitted across his features, everything from anger to surprise to sadness. "I never really thought about it, but I guess I do carry some anger toward her. But ultimately I'm sad I didn't get to know her. My grandmother told me wonderful stories about her."

"It sounds like Winnie and your granddad were here for you."

"Yes. That's why I feel like I'm letting Winnie down."

"How so?"

"I pursued my own interests and became a marine biologist, but there's a part of me that enjoys watching my grandmother create a product. I had a double major in chemistry and marine biology, but I went on to get my doctorate in marine biology because that interested me the most. I got the chemistry degree for my grandparents, but I did like the field."

"Then why did you become a marine biologist?"

"To see what I could accomplish alone, without the Winfield name." His mouth lifted in a lopsided grin. "How about you? What were your parents like?"

She'd wanted to get to know Colt better and should have realized he would want to do the same. "I don't talk about my childhood. It's behind me. Not something I care to revisit."

One of his eyebrows rose. "I should share my whole life story with you, but yours is off-limits?"

"I said I don't talk about it, but I'll make an exception with you."

"Why?"

"Because…" She didn't know how to say what she felt was developing between them because she had never been good at relationships. She was better as a loner, and her job made that easier.

"Because of what's happening between us?"

"What is that?" *Help me to understand.*

He shifted toward her, crowding her space. "I wish I knew. I do know I'm attracted to you. That if our circumstances were different, we could be friends—good friends. Maybe…" He swallowed hard.

"More?"

He nodded. "You feel it, too?"

"Yes. But you're right. Our lives are in different parts of the world and—"

He bent forward and kissed her hard, cutting off her words, robbing her of a decent breath. But she didn't care. She returned his kiss with her own fervent feelings. Intense, overwhelming. Threatening her emotionally.

She pulled back, one part of her not wanting to end the kiss, but the sensible part of her demanding she act now before she surrendered her heart to Colt. "You know, all this talk has worn me out. I'd better do my rounds then go to bed."

She got to her feet and put some space between them before he coaxed her to stay. He wouldn't have to say much. She skirted around the coffee table and started for the hallway.

"Ellie."

She turned toward him.

"I'm a good listener. When you want to talk about your parents, I'm here."

She strode across the foyer, making sure the alarm system was on and working. Then she began with the dining room, examining the windows to verify they were locked. Not many people had ever told her they would listen to her about her past, but then she'd rarely given anyone the chance. Colt was scaling the walls she kept up around herself. Was it time to let him in?

* * *

Late the next afternoon, not long before the sun went down, Ellie propped her shoulder against a post on the porch of the mountain cabin. The Winfield place was nothing like the image of a tiny log cabin she had in her mind. Though the bottom portion was made out of logs, the three-bedroom A-frame was huge and imposing. The smoke from the huge stone fireplace, its wisps entwining with the falling snow, scented the crisp air. A large mug with Linda's delicious hot chocolate, which she'd sent with them before they'd climbed into the four-wheel-drive Jeep and trekked up to the top of the mountain, warmed her bare hands.

The cabin door opened and closed. Colt came to stand beside her with his own drink. "It's beautiful up here. The view when it isn't snowing is breathtaking."

"Will this snow be a problem?"

"The weather report says this system should move out fairly fast. We'll probably get six or seven inches. Nothing we can't handle. But we have enough food for four or five days. We always come prepared with almost twice what we need and there are staples left up here. Doug and Linda use the cabin throughout the year."

"I was glad to see you had a landline. I knew the cell reception was nonexistent this far up the mountain. I don't want to be totally cut off from civilization."

"Mary Ann can't hurt Winnie anymore. The ME ruled it a suicide, and the sheriff couldn't find anything to indicate she wasn't working alone. Winnie is tickled they have a lead on where the dogs could have been sold."

"That'll be a nice Christmas present for Winnie if they find the dogs and they're back at the estate when she comes down off the mountain."

"If it's possible, Sheriff Quinn and Doug will make it happen."

"Winnie has a lot of people who care about her and watch out for her. That says a lot about her."

Colt's gaze snared hers. "How about you? You told me once your brother died when you were young. Do you have any more siblings?"

"Nope. It was just him and me. He was my twin."

"That had to be extra hard on you."

"Yes it was. He had a congenital heart defect that finally got the best of him."

"How old were you?"

"Thirteen."

"How were your parents?"

Suddenly the cold seemed to seep through the layers of clothing Ellie wore. She shivered, taking a large swallow of the now lukewarm chocolate. "I'd better go back inside before I freeze."

In the cabin, Winnie sat in a chair before the fire, knitting. Ellie stopped a few feet into the great room.

Winnie glanced up. "These past few years I haven't gotten to knit like I used to. I found my needles and some yarn and decided to see if I remembered how." A smile curved her mouth, her hands moving quickly.

"It looks like you remember."

"Yes. A nice surprise. The second I stepped inside the cabin I felt like a new woman. My product line is finished, at least for the time being, and the person after me has been found. I'd say that was a wonderful Christmas gift." She lifted the patch of yarn. "And now this. Have you ever knitted?"

Laughing, Ellie took the chair across from her. "I wouldn't be able to sit still long enough to do it. That's something I'll leave to others."

"I might just make this into a scarf for you. That way you won't forget me when you get back to Dallas and go onto another assignment."

"Forget you?" Ellie shook her head. "That's not gonna happen. You're an amazing woman."

A hint of red colored her cheeks. "Where's my grandson?"

"Communing with nature," Ellie said with a shrug.

"I'm glad you didn't change your mind about coming." Winnie paused and leaned toward her, lowering her voice. "I was sure you would."

"Why?"

"I saw you yesterday while we were decorating and celebrating. You weren't totally comfortable with the whole scene. I imagine since you go from one place to another because of your job, you don't do much for the holidays. Who did you spend Thanksgiving with this year?"

"No one. I microwaved a turkey dinner and celebrated alone. I have a standing invitation to Kyra's, but I hate always intruding on her and her husband. They're practically newlyweds."

"Kind of painful sometimes being around a couple deeply in love when you aren't."

"That's not it. I just…" *Just what?* she asked herself. In truth, Winnie was probably right. Kyra and Michael were always so good to include her in whatever they were doing, but she saw the looks exchanged between them—full of love that excluded everyone else in the room. She'd never had a man look at her like that—not even Greg, who she had thought she would marry one day. "It's not that I want a relationship, but there are times I get lonely."

"We all do. And why don't you want a relationship? You have a lot to offer a man."

Ellie peered at the front door, relieved it was still closed and Colt was outside. "I don't think I'd be very good at it. I've always depended on myself for everything."

"Everything? Not God a little bit?"

"Well, yes. I know He's there, but I'm not sure He's that interested in my day-to-day life."

"Oh, He is."

"Then where was He when I was growing up? Having to raise myself? Take care of my brother because our mother couldn't be bothered?" She finally said the questions that had plagued her ever since she gave herself to Christ.

"Look at the type of woman you've grown into. You're strong. You can take care of yourself. You help others have peace of mind when trouble happens in their life. I for one am thankful you came into my life. Sadly, an easy road doesn't usually hone a person into what they need to be."

The door finally opened, and Colt hurried inside, stomping his feet. Snow covered his hair and coat. "I forgot something in the Jeep and went out to get it." After shrugging out of his heavy jacket, he put a sack on the table near the chair he settled into. "It's really snowing now.

Too much more and we'll have whiteout conditions."

"It sounds like the weatherman got it wrong." Ellie eyed the bag. "What did you forget?"

"A surprise."

"You know a bodyguard doesn't like surprises."

"This is a good one." He quirked a grin, his eyes sparkling. "You and Winnie have to wait until Christmas morning."

"It's a present? I didn't get you anything." An edge of panic invaded Ellie's voice. A gift from him made their…friendship even more personal.

"It's nothing. And I don't want anything. That's not why I'm giving you this."

Winnie laughed. "Ellie, enjoy it. Colt loves giving gifts. He's just like his grandfather. I used to be able to find out what it was before Colt gave it to me. But not anymore. He's gotten quite good at keeping a secret."

"So, Winnie, what are we having for dinner?" Colt combed his fingers through his wet hair.

Winnie gave him a look. "Are you suffering from hypothermia? You want *me* to fix dinner?"

Colt chuckled. "Not if I want to eat anything decent. I was teasing you. Ellie and I will cook dinner for you." He rose and offered Ellie his hand.

She took it and let him tug her up. "You do

know I don't cook a lot for myself. I'm not home that much."

"But I cook. We all take turns on the ship, and if we weren't accomplished, we quickly learned or the rest of the crew threatened to toss us overboard."

Ellie examined the contents of the refrigerator. "Grilling is out," she said as she glanced back at Colt. "Which, by the way, I am good at. So I guess the steaks can wait for a less snowy day."

"From the looks of it outside, I don't know that's going to happen before we leave. We can use the broiler in the oven."

"So how are we going to get out of here if it snows that much?"

"We have a snowmobile in the shed out back and skis."

"Winnie skis?"

"She did when she was younger, but she'll use the snowmobile. How are you on skis?"

"Never tried it. I live in flat country."

"We have some cross-country skis. Flat country is fine for that."

"But the way down isn't flat. I might not make a pretty picture on skis, but I'll do what I have to." She took the meat out of the refrigerator. "Okay, steak it is. I can actually prepare them and put them in the broiler. So what are you gonna cook?"

His chuckle spiced the air. "I see how this is going to go. I'm going to do most of the work. I thought you said you could cook."

"Simple things like steaks. Let's say you're the head chef and I'm the assistant. Believe me, you all will be much better off."

"Well then, let's make this simple. Baked potatoes and a salad."

"I'm all for easy."

Surprisingly Ellie found they cooked well as a team, and by the time they sat down to eat she'd laughed more at the stories Colt told her about life on the research vessel than she had in a long time. Her jobs were serious and left little room for the lighter side of life.

"I'm glad you two talked me into coming up here," Ellie said when Winnie finished her blessing. "I've worked a lot in the past few years and have had little downtime. I needed this and didn't even realize it. No bad guys out there stalking a client. That's a nice feeling"

Winnie agreed. "That's how I'm looking at these next three days. A minivacation that I needed a lot. I'm too old to work as hard as I have been with Endless Youth. But it's mostly done, and I've accomplished what Thomas and I set out to do all those years ago. Once the company goes public, I'm stepping down as CEO of Glamour Sensations."

Colt dropped his fork on his plate. "You're finally retiring? I've been wanting you to slow down for years."

Winnie pursed her lips. "I would have if a certain young grandson had decided to use his degree in chemistry and come into the business. I figure Harold can take over the CEO position until he grooms someone for the job."

Ellie picked up on the sudden tension that thickened at the table between grandson and grandmother. She swallowed her bite of mushroom-covered steak and said, "What are you going to do with all your free time?"

"I won't completely turn the company over without keeping an eye on it. But I figure I could knit, read, wait for great-grandchildren."

Colt's eyes popped wide. "Winnie, now I know why you insisted on coming up here. Did you have something to do with all this snow, too? We won't be going anywhere until it stops. Visibility is limited."

His grandmother smiled. "I have a lot of skills, but controlling weather isn't one of them. I figured the circumstances were just right for me telling you this now rather than right before you go back to the *Kaleidoscope*. You'll inherit my shares in the company so you'll have a stake in it."

"What's this about great-grandchildren? This is the first time you've bought that up in a long time."

Winnie pointedly looked at Ellie before swinging her attention to Colt. "Just a little reminder. After all, I'm getting up there. These threats made me realize I won't be around forever. I need to make plans for the future."

Colt's eyebrows slashed downward, and he lowered his head, as though he was enthralled with cutting his steak.

"The threat is over and you should have many years before you, Winnie," Ellie said, trying to defuse the tension vibrating in the air.

"I'm planning on it, but it's in the Lord's hands."

The rest of the meal Winnie and Ellie mostly talked, with a few comments from Colt. What part of the conversation had upset him? Ellie wondered. The part about Harold becoming CEO or the great-grandchildren?

At the end Ellie rose. "I'll take care of the dishes. That I know how to do at least. When I was first in the army I was on mess duty a lot."

"Colt will help you," Winnie offered. "You're our guest. We certainly can't let you do it alone."

As Ellie walked into the kitchen she heard

Colt say in a strained voice, "I know what you're doing, and you need to stop it."

"Stop what? If you want, I'll help her."

The sugary sweet sound of Winnie's voice alerted Ellie to the fact that the woman was up to something, and she had a pretty good idea what it was. When Colt came into the small kitchen, his expression reflected his irritated mood toward his grandmother. Ellie worked beside him in silence for ten minutes.

As she washed the broiler pan, she asked, "What's going on with you and Winnie? Are you upset about her retiring and Harold taking over?" She didn't think that was it.

"I'm glad she's retiring, and Harold's a good man. Don't tell her, but lately I've been thinking about what I need to do. I don't see me living on a research vessel for years."

"So you might help with the company?"

"Maybe. I have an obligation that I need to finish first to the research team."

"Then what has you upset? And don't tell me you aren't. It's all over your face."

"She hasn't played the great-grandchildren card in ages. I thought she'd learned her lesson the last time."

"What lesson?"

"Come on. You're smart. Don't you see she's trying to play matchmaker with us?"

"It did cross my mind, but I think it's cute."

"Cute! The last time she did, I went out with the woman to make her happy. On the surface she seemed all right until we stopped dating and she began stalking me. That's one of the reasons I took the job on the *Kaleidoscope*. It's hard to stalk a person in the middle of the Pacific Ocean. It turns out I've enjoyed the work I'm doing and the woman went on to marry and move to New York, but Winnie isn't usually that far off reading people."

"We're all entitled to a mistake every once in a while. Besides, she had your best interests at heart—at least in her mind."

"I told the lady I wasn't interested in a serious relationship. She was and didn't understand why I wasn't. Hence the stalking to discover why she wasn't Mrs. Right."

"Don't worry. I don't stalk. I protect people from stalkers. And I'm not interested in a serious relationship, either. So you're perfectly safe. Your grandmother's wiles won't work on me." Ellie wiped down the sink. "So if you know that your grandmother has done that in the past, why did you talk me into coming this morning when I voiced an objection?"

He blew out a frustrated breath. "Because I like you. I've enjoyed getting to know you, and I didn't like the idea that you would spend Christmas alone."

"Oh, I see."

"Do you? Winnie needs to realize a man can have a friendship with a woman. She keeps insisting Harold is just a friend, so surely she can understand we can be friends."

Ellie laughed. "You don't have to convince me. Just Winnie."

"Yeah. Besides, after Christmas, I'll go back to *Kaleidoscope* and you'll go on another assignment. We'll probably be halfway around the world from each other."

"I agree. Forgive the cliché, but we're like two ships passing in the night."

"Exactly." He draped the dish towel over the handle on the oven. "And I think I'll go in there and explain it to her. Want to back me up?"

"Sure."

Colt stalked into the great room and found it empty. He turned in a full circle, his gaze falling on the knitting project in the basket by the chair his grandmother had been sitting in. His forehead crinkled, and he covered the distance to the hall, coming back almost immediately. "She went to bed. It's just you and me, and it's only nine o'clock."

"I think that was her intention."

"I know." A chuckle escaped Colt. "And I'll

have a serious word with her tomorrow. In the meantime, want to play chess or checkers?"

"I can't play chess, so it has to be checkers."

Colt retrieved the board and game pieces and set it up at the table where they had eaten their dinner. "I'll have to teach you how to play chess. It's a strategy game. I have a feeling you'd be good at it."

"Maybe tomorrow. After the past few weeks, I don't want too tough a game to play tonight." Ellie took a chair across from him. "After an assignment I go through a mental and physical letdown, and after a particularly hard job, I almost shut down for a couple of days."

"Is this your way of telling me you're going to lounge around and do nothing but eat bonbons?"

"If you have any, I might. I like chocolate." Ellie moved her red checker forward.

"What else do you like?" Colt made his play, then looked up into her eyes, trapping her with the intensity in his gaze. Electrifying. Mesmerizing.

"Protecting people," she somehow managed to reply. "I really do like my work. Making sure a place is secure. Trying to figure out all the ways a person can get to another."

"I can understand liking your job. I like mine, too."

"What do you like about your job?"

"Finding unique species. Trying to preserve the ocean. The challenge of the job. That's probably what I like the most. I want a job that forces me beyond my comfort zone."

"We have a lot in common."

Colt answered her move by jumping her red checker. "You said you became a bodyguard because you want to help those who need protection. Why is that important to you?"

"King me," Ellie said when she slid her first red piece into his home base. "Because my twin was bullied. I wasn't going to allow that to happen to others if I could do something about it."

"He was but you weren't?"

"No. I had a rep for being tough and not taking anything from anyone."

He cocked his head to the side. "How did you get that reputation?"

"By standing up to the people who made fun of my brother. Toby was slow. He was the second twin. He became stuck in the birth canal and was deprived of oxygen, which caused some medical and mental problems."

"When did you start championing him like that?"

"When we started school. Kindergarten."

"What did your parents think?"

Ellie looked at the board and made a move without thinking it through. With his next turn,

Colt jumped her pieces until she had to crown his black checker.

"Obviously the subject of your parents isn't one of your favorites," he said. "Like me."

Ellie swallowed the tightness in her throat. Recalling her past never sat well with her. "No. I never knew my father. He left my mother when Toby and I were born. He never once tried to get in touch with us. And for different reasons from your dad, my mother was less than stellar in the parent department. I basically raised Toby and myself. I didn't have grandparents like yours."

"So you and I have another thing in common."

There was something about Colt that drew her. She hadn't wanted to admit that to herself, but she couldn't avoid it any longer. They were alike in a lot of ways even though their backgrounds were very different. He came from wealth and was college educated. She'd graduated from high school and had been educated on the job in the army.

Ten minutes later Colt won the checkers game. She wanted to think it was because her mind hadn't been on the game, but that wasn't true. He was good and she wasn't. She hadn't played since she was a kid and the old man next door used to challenge her. She hadn't won then, either, but she had enjoyed her neighbor's conversation about the different places she could see around the world. So when the U.S. Army recruiter came to her school, she'd thought it would be a good way to go different places.

"Another game?" Colt asked.

"No, one beating in a night is enough. My ego can only take so much."

He threw back his head and laughed. "I have a feeling your ego is just fine."

"Okay, I hate to admit that Winnie has the right idea about going to bed early. What's even nicer is that I don't have to walk through the house and check to make sure we are locked up tight. No one in their right mind would come out on a night like this." Ellie made her way to the window and opened the blinds to look at the heavy snow coming down.

"Near blizzard conditions," Colt said close to her ear.

The tickle of his breath on her nape zipped through her, but she stayed still. There was nothing stopping her from turning around and kissing him. No job. No threats against Winnie. This was her time that she'd chosen to spend with Winnie and Colt. His presence so near to her tingled her nerve endings and charged her, demanding she put aside her exhaustion and give in to the feelings bombarding her from all sides.

"Yes, I haven't seen this much snow in a while." Her reply ended in a breathless rush.

"It makes this cabin feel even cozier." His soft, whispered words caressed her neck.

She tensed, trying to keep herself from leaning back against him.

"Relax. We'll be perfectly fine in here. If we need rescuing, people know where we are and will come when we don't show up the day after Christmas."

His teasing tone coaxed the tension from her. She closed the blind and swung around at the same time she stepped away. "I think I can survive being snowbound in a large, warm cabin with enough food for a week. My boss doesn't expect me to come into the office until the day after New Year's."

"I wish I could say the same thing. I have to get back to the ship."

His comment reminded her of their differences. She was a bodyguard. He worked on a vessel in the middle of the Pacific Ocean. Not conducive to a relationship. "Good night, Colt."

"Coward."

"Oh, you think?" She'd been accused of being many things. Being a coward wasn't one of them.

"When it gets personal, you leave."

"That's what this is?" She drew a circle in the air to indicate where they were standing.

He moved to the side, sweeping his arm across his body. "Good night, Ellie. We'll continue our conversation tomorrow when you're rested."

On her way to her bedroom, the searing heat of his gaze drilled into her back. Every inch of her was aware of the man she'd wanted to kiss but didn't. It was better this way. Now she only had a few more days and she could escape to Dallas.

Ellie hurriedly changed into her sweatpants and large T-shirt then fell into bed. She expected sleep to come quickly. But she couldn't stop thinking about Colt. At some point she must have gone to sleep because the next thing she realized a boom shook the cabin, sending her flying out of bed.

Chapter Ten

Ellie fumbled in the dark for her gun she kept on the nightstand out of habit. When her fingers clasped around it, she raced into the hallway at the same time Colt came out of his bedroom.

"Check on Winnie," she said and hurried into the great room. The cabin seemed intact, but when she peered toward the large window that overlooked the front of the place, she saw an orange-yellow glow through the slats in the blinds as though the sun had set in the yard. She yanked open the door, a blast of cold rushing in while flames engulfed the Jeep nearby in the still-falling snow.

Gun up, she moved out onto the porch. When she stepped into the snow blown up against the cabin, she glanced down and realized she had no shoes on. In spite of the biting cold battering her, she scanned the white terrain. Although night, it was light and eerie. The storm had died down some but still raged, as did the fire where the Jeep was.

From behind a hand clamped on her shoulder. She jerked around, her gun automatically coming up.

Colt's eyes grew round, his hand falling back to his side.

"Don't ever come up behind me like that, especially after something like this." Using her weapon, she gestured toward the flames. "I could have shot you."

With her toes freezing and the sensation spreading up her legs, she hotfooted it into the cabin and shut the door, locking it. "How's Winnie?"

"I'm fine."

Ellie glanced over Colt's shoulder. Winnie hovered near the hallway, wrapped in a quilt. "You know what this means."

She nodded. "Mary Ann didn't send those threats."

"Possibly. Or someone was working with her and maybe killed her to keep her quiet. It's possible to make a murder look like suicide. That's what the police wanted to determine when her body was discovered."

"The Jeep couldn't have exploded on its own?" Winnie came farther into the room.

"Not likely."

Colt parted a few slats on the blinds and peeked outside. "The fire is dying down with all the snow falling, and the wind has, too. We need to call the sheriff."

Ellie marched to the phone and picked it up. "No dial tone. This is definitely not an accident."

"So we're trapped in this cabin with no way to get help." Colt strode into the kitchen and peered out the window. "I see nothing on this side."

Ellie checked the other sides of the cabin, calling out from her bedroom, "Clear here." *For the time being.*

"What do we do? Who is behind this?" Winnie's voice quavered.

Ellie reentered the great room. "At the moment the who isn't important. We need to come up with a plan. If he blew up the Jeep, he could try something with the cabin and we can't guard all four sides 24/7. He might have destroyed the Jeep to get us out of the house."

"How can we leave?" Winnie pulled the blanket closer to her.

"The snow is starting to let up," Colt said. "Maybe I could make it down the mountain and get help. You could stay here with Winnie and guard her. I know these mountains and have the best chance of getting out of here."

Ellie faced Colt. "How are you going to walk out of here? Over a foot of snow was dumped on us in the past twelve hours."

"We have snowshoes I can use. Or I'll get to the snowmobile in the shed and use that."

"What if he's out there waiting to shoot anyone who leaves?" This was a situation where she wished she were two people and could stay and protect but also go and get help.

He clasped her arms. "I've fought off pirates. I can do this. Besides, the visibility isn't good because it's still night and snowing."

"Exactly. It won't be good for you, either." Thinking about what could happen to him knotted her stomach.

"But I know this area well. I doubt the person out there does. This is Winfield land. Not much else is up here. This isn't debatable. I'm going. You're staying." A determined expression carved harsh lines into his face.

She nodded. She didn't like the plan, but they didn't have a choice.

Colt started for his bedroom.

Winnie stepped into his path. "Colt, don't do this. I don't like you being a target for this person. You're my only family left."

"I have to go. I'm taking Granddad's handgun

with me." He looked back at Ellie. "I'm leaving his rifle in case you need it."

"Fine. Bring it out here with ammunition. I'll keep you covered for as long as I can." The helplessness Ellie experienced festered inside her. Protection was her job, not his.

Winnie turned large eyes on Ellie as Colt disappeared down the hallway. "I'm glad Thomas taught Colt to shoot. At that time it was for him to protect himself if he came upon a bear or cougar in these mountains—not a person bent on killing me."

"You won't die as long as I have a breath in me." Ellie's hands curled into fists.

Nor Colt. I won't let him die, either. He means too much to me. That realization stunned her for a moment, then because she had no choice, she shoved it into the background. She couldn't risk her emotions getting in the way of whatever she had to do.

When he reemerged from the hallway, dressed in a heavy overcoat and wool beanie, carrying snowshoes, thick gloves, goggles and the rifle, he thrust the latter into Ellie's hand then dug for a box of shells and laid them on a nearby table. "More ammunition is on top of my bureau."

He put on his goggles, wrapped a scarf around his neck and lower face, donned his snowshoes and gloves, then eased the back door open. Cracking a window that overlooked the back of the cabin, she took up guard as Colt trudged his way toward the shed two hundred feet away.

Her nerves taut, she shouldered the rifle, poised to fire if she needed to. Ellie scoped the terrain for anything that moved. All was still. Not even the branches of the pine trees swayed from wind now.

"What's happening? I don't hear the snowmobile," Winnie said behind Ellie.

"Nothing. He's inside the shed." *But is he safe?* What if the assailant was waiting for him? Ellie couldn't leave Winnie. That might be what the person wanted. But what if Colt needed—

The side door to the shed opened, and Colt hurried back toward the house, his gaze scanning the area.

"What happened?" Ellie asked at the same time Winnie did when Colt reentered the cabin.

"The snowmobile won't start. Someone disabled it."

"Are you sure? Does it have gas?"

"There's a hole in the tank. The gas leaked out all over the ground. The ski equipment and anything else we might use to leave here is gone. He's cut us off."

Trapped. She'd been trapped before and gotten out. She would this time, too, with both

Colt and Winnie. "Okay. For the time being let's fortify the cabin, find places to watch our surroundings while we figure out what we should do."

"I still think I should try leaving here on foot," Colt insisted.

"Maybe. What's up in the loft?" Ellie pointed to a narrow staircase.

"Storage mostly, but it might be a better vantage place to watch the area from," Colt said.

"I'm going to fix some coffee. We need to stay alert. I don't think there's going to be any more sleep tonight."

"Thanks, Winnie. I could use a whole pot." Colt kissed his grandmother on the check.

When she left, Ellie moved toward the stairs. "Keep an eye on her while I look at the loft."

Colt stepped closer and whispered, "Ellie, I don't think Winnie could make it out of here, so all three of us going is not an option. She might have power walked around the perimeter of the estate, but sloshing through the deep snow even with snowshoes is totally different. It's exhausting after a few hundred yards. And snowshoeing can be treacherous going downhill over rough terrain, especially with her weak knees. Not to mention leaving her exposed for the person to shoot."

"And you don't think you'll be."

"What's the alternative? Waiting until we're missed? That could be days. No telling what would happen in that time."

"I'll be back down in a few minutes. Check the windows and doors to make sure they're locked. Put some heavy furniture up against the two doors. Shutter the windows we won't use for a lookout."

"What are you two whispering about?" Poised in the entrance into the kitchen, Winnie planted her fists on her waist. "If you're worried about me, let me inform you I'll do what I have to. I won't let this person win. Any planning and discussions need to include me. Understand?"

Ellie exchanged a glance with Colt before he pivoted and headed toward his grandmother, saying, "We were just discussing our options."

Ellie clambered up the stairs. The whole loft was one large room with boxes and pieces of furniture stored along the walls. Two big windows overlooked the west and east part of the landscape. One person with little effort could keep an eye on over half the terrain. That could leave Winnie and Colt covering the north and south. That might work. But then as she started back down the stairs, questions and doubts began tumbling through her mind like a skier who lost her balance going down a mountain.

The scent of coffee lured her toward the

kitchen. She poured a mug and joined Winnie in the great room before the dying fire. She gave the older woman a smile, hoping to cajole one from her.

But Winnie's frown deepened. "I've been trying to figure out who would go to such lengths to get me. I honestly can't imagine anything I've done to cause this kind of hatred. I feel so helpless."

Ellie remembered that exact feeling a little while ago. It never sat well with her. "I've been thinking."

Colt suddenly came from the hallway with his arms full of warm clothing, snowshoes and other items. "If we need to leave suddenly, I want this on hand. I'm separating it into piles for each of us."

"I say we have two options. All of us leave and try to make it down the mountain. Or I go by myself and bring help back." Ellie sat on the edge of the sofa, every sense attuned to her surroundings.

"Those aren't two options in my opinion," Colt said. "I'm going it alone. I can move fast. I should be able to get back with help by dark if I leave right away. The best place for me to try and get to is the estate. I think that's the best—"

"No, Colt. You're not going by yourself. I won't have you get killed because of me. There is a third option. We stay here. That's what I want." Winnie pinched her lips together and pointedly looked at each one of them.

Colt surged to his feet. "Sorry. I love you, Winnie, but the longer we spread this out the more this person has a chance to accomplish what he wants to do. Kill you and in the process take us all out."

"I agree with Colt about us all waiting, but I'd rather be the one going for help. I know how to avoid being a human target. I was trained in that."

"Winnie is your client and first priority."

"I know. That's the dilemma I—"

Thump!

"What was that?" Ellie rose and started for the window by the front door. She motioned Colt to check the back area.

Again she heard the sound—like something striking the side of the cabin. Ellie parted the blinds to peer outside. Nothing unusual but the sight of the charred Jeep.

Thump!

"That's coming from the north side." Colt rushed down the hallway.

Ellie helped Winnie to her feet and followed him. "Do you see anything?"

He whirled from the window. "We've got to

get out of here. He's firing flaming arrows at the cabin."

Ellie stared out at the evergreen forest, which afforded a lot of cover along the north area of the property. Another arrow rocketed toward the cabin, landing on the roof. "He's burning us out. Either we leave or die in a fire."

Colt ushered them out of the room. "Let's go. If we can get away, I think I know a place you two can hide. It's defensible, only one way in. We need to dress as warm as possible."

"He's on the north side. We'll use the window facing south to get out of here. He can't watch all four sides at once."

Winnie halted before her pile of garments. "Unless there is more than one."

"We have to take our chances and pray the Lord protects us." Ellie quickly dressed, then stuffed useful items into a backpack—flashlights, a blanket, matches, weapons, some bottled water and food.

"He'll be able to track us, but the cave system isn't too far away and it's beginning to snow again. I hope the conditions worsen after we get to the cave. The way I have to go is down. I can do that even in less-than-favorable visibility." Colt prepared his backpack then slung it over one shoulder.

The noise of the arrows hitting the cabin increased. The scent of smoke drifted to Ellie as they hurried into the laundry room. A three-by-three window four feet off the floor beckoned her. She pulled a chair to it and opened their escape route. A blast of cold air and snow invaded the warmth of the small room.

Ellie stuck her head out the opening. It was at least six feet to the ground. "I'll go first, then you, Winnie. Colt can help lower you to me."

After tossing her backpack out the hole, Ellie leaped up and shimmied through the small space, diving headfirst and tucking into a ball. The snow cushioned her tumble to the ground. She bounced up and positioned herself to guide Winnie, breaking her fall. While Colt wiggled through the opening and followed Ellie's example, she and Winnie put on their snowshoes. Colt donned his as fast as he could.

The thumping sound thundered through the air.

Winnie started to say something. Ellie put her finger up to her mouth. Colt's grandmother nodded that she understood.

Colt pointed in the direction he would take, then set out in a slow pace with Winnie mirroring his steps, then Ellie. The less snow they disturbed the faster the falling flakes would cover their tracks.

When Colt reached the edge of the forest that

surrounded the cabin, Ellie paused and glanced back. The stench of smoke hung in the air, but she couldn't see any wisps of it coming from the cabin because of the heavy snowfall. Even the indentations they'd made were filling in, though still evident.

Then the sound of the arrows striking the cabin stopped. Ellie searched the white landscape but saw no sign of the assailant. She turned forward and hurried as fast as she could to catch up with Colt and Winnie.

Fifteen minutes later, the wind began whipping through the trees, bringing biting cold to penetrate their layers of clothing. Even with so little skin exposed to the chill, Ellie shivered and gritted her teeth to keep them from chattering.

A cracking noise reverberated through the forest, followed by a crash to their left. Ellie looked up at the snow-and ice-burdened limbs on the pines and realized the danger of being beneath the heavy-laden branches. Winnie barely picked up each foot as she moved forward. Her pace slowed even more.

When Winnie stumbled and fell, Ellie whispered, "Colt," and rushed toward the woman.

The wind whisked his name away. He kept trudging forward.

"Colt," she said a little louder as she bent over

to help Winnie to her feet, one snowshoe coming off.

He glanced back, saw his grandmother down and retraced his steps as quickly as he could. He assisted Winnie to her feet while Ellie knelt and tied the snowshoe back on Winnie's foot. Snow-covered, the older woman shook.

Another crack, like a gun going off, resonated in the air. A pine branch snapped above them and plunged toward them. Ellie dove into both Colt and Winnie, sending them flying to the side. The limb struck the ground a foot away from them.

Dazed, Winnie lay in the snow, then pain flashed across her face.

"What's wrong, Winnie?" Ellie asked, pushing up onto her hands and knees next to the woman.

"I think I did something to my ankle," she murmured, her voice barely audible over the howl of the wind through the trees.

Colt knelt next to Winnie. "I'll carry you the rest of the way. The cave isn't far."

"I'm so sorry, Winnie." Ellie peered at the large branch on the ground.

"Don't you apologize. I could have been hurt a lot worse if that had fallen on me."

While Colt scooped up his grandmother, Ellie used her knife to cut a small branch off the big one. She used the pine to smooth out the snow behind them as much as possible and hide their tracks.

Ten minutes later, Colt mounted a rocky surface, went around a large boulder and stooped to enter a cave. Ellie stayed back to clear away their steps as much as possible, then went inside the dark cavern, reaching for her flashlight to illuminate the area. A damp, musky odor prevailed.

Colt set his grandmother on the floor, took a blanket out of his backpack and spread it out, then moved Winnie to it. Kneeling, he removed the boot from the injured foot and examined it. "The ankle's starting to swell. I don't think it's broken. But a doctor will have to look at it when we get home. The faster I leave, the faster you'll get the medical care you need."

Ellie slung her backpack to the ground near Winnie and sat on it. "We'll be fine. I'll make Winnie comfortable then stand guard near the entrance."

"I should be back before dark. If I can get to the house, I can get help. It's a little out of the way, but I think it would save time in the long run. I know I can find help there." Colt started to stand.

Winnie grabbed his arm. "I love you. Don't you dare take any more risks than you absolutely have to. If you have to take your time to be safe, then you've got to do that."

"Yes, ma'am." He kissed her forehead. "I have a good reason to make it safely down the mountain."

Ellie rose and walked with him a few feet. "Ditto what your grandmother said. I have food and water. We have a couple of blankets. We'll be fine." She tied his scarf, which had come loose, back around his neck. Suddenly emotions jammed her throat. She knew the dangers in store for Colt. Not just the rough terrain in a snowstorm but a maniac bent on killing them.

He clasped her glove-covered hands and bent his head toward hers. A smile graced his mouth right before his lips grazed across hers once then twice. Then he kissed her fully. She returned it with all her needs and concerns pouring into the connection that sprang up between them.

In a raw whisper, she said against his mouth, "Don't you dare get hurt. We have things to talk about when this is over."

"If I hadn't been motivated before, I am now." He gave her a quick peck on her lips then departed, striding toward the cave entrance.

Ellie watched him vanish around the corner, then went back to Winnie to make sure she was comfortable before she stood guard at the mouth of the cavern.

"He'll be all right," Winnie assured her. "He knows these mountains well. Hopefully better than whoever is after me."

Ellie nodded at Winnie, remembering the grin Colt gave her before kissing her. The memory warmed her cold insides. "Yes. After all, he's fought off pirates before."

Winnie chuckled.

The warmth died out when a gunshot blasted the air and the mountain over them rumbled.

Chapter Eleven

Colt exited the cave, scanning the terrain for any sign of their assailant. Through the curtain of snow falling a movement caught his full attention. Suddenly a shadow rose from behind a rock and aimed a rifle at him. Colt dove for cover as the white-camouflaged figure got off a shot, the bullet ricocheting off the stone surface behind him.

A noise rocked the ground—like a huge wave hitting shore in a thunderstorm. Colt had only heard that sound one other time, right before tons of snow crashed down the mountain, plowing through the forest, leaving nothing behind in its wake.

The entrance of the cave a few feet away was his only chance. He scrambled toward it as rock, snow and ice began pelting him.

* * *

Winnie went white. "An avalanche!"

Ellie hurried toward the entrance. "Stay put," she said, realizing Winnie didn't have a choice.

As she rounded the bend in the stone corridor, she saw Colt plunge toward the cave, then a wall of white swallowed him up. The force of the avalanche sent a swell of snow mushrooming into the cavern.

When the rumbling stopped, snow totally blocked the cave entrance and she couldn't see Colt. She rushed to the last place he'd been and began digging with her hands. Cold and wet invaded the warmth of her gloves, leaving her hands freezing. She didn't care. Nor did she care Winnie and she were trapped. She had to find Colt.

Please, Lord, let me find him. Please.

Over and over those words zoomed through her mind.

But all she uncovered was more snow.

Stunned, with limited oxygen, Colt tried to unfurl his body so he could use his hands to dig his way out before he lost consciousness. But the snow encased him in a cold coffin. He had a small pocket of air, but it wouldn't last long. He finally dislodged his arm from beneath him and reached it toward the direction of the cave, but he could move it only a few inches.

Lord, help me. Winnie and Ellie are in danger.

"I'm in here," he called out, hoping that Ellie was free on the other side.

"Colt!"

The sound of Ellie's voice gave him hope she could dig him out before he ran out of oxygen. "I'm here."

"I can hear you, Colt. Hang on."

He focused on those words and tried to calm his rapid heartbeat, to even his breathing in order to preserve his air. A peace settled around him as if God enclosed him in an embrace.

"Ellie, what happened?" Winnie called out. "It sounded like an avalanche."

"It was. I'm assessing our situation." Ellie kept digging near the area where she'd heard Colt and prayed he wasn't buried too deeply.

If he was almost to the entrance of the cave, he would have been sheltered from the worst of the avalanche. Concerned for Colt, she hadn't thought about their situation till now. They were trapped in the cave. It would be days before a search party was sent out, and then would the rescuers even realize they were trapped in the cavern? And if they did, would it be in time? She had a couple of water bottles and a little food, but what worried her the most was the cold. A chill infused every crevice of the cave.

Although tired from shoveling the snow with her hands, she didn't dare take a break. "Colt, are you there?"

"Yes," his faint response came back and a surge of adrenaline pumped energy through her body.

Her hand broke through the snow and touched him, and relief trembled down her length. She doubled her attack as though sand was running out of an hourglass and she only had seconds left to free him. Soon his arm was revealed. He wiggled it to let her know he was okay. She kept going, uncovering more of him until he could assist her.

When he escaped the mound of snow, Ellie helped him to stand, then engulfed him in her arms. "Are you all right? Hurt anywhere?"

"I feel like an elephant—no, several—sat on me, but other than that, I'm in one piece."

She leaned back to look into his dear face, one she had thought she would never see again. "I heard a gunshot then the rumble of the avalanche. What happened?"

"Our assailant found us and shot at me when I came out of the cave. That must have triggered the avalanche. I dove back into the cave. He might not have been so fortunate."

"Then he could be buried under tons of snow?"

"It'll depend on where he was and how fast he reacted, but it's definitely a possibility."

"Come on. Winnie is worried." Ellie grasped his gloved hand in hers and relished the connection. She'd almost lost him. That thought forced her to acknowledge her growing feelings toward Colt. There was no time to dwell on them now, but she would have to in the future. Every day she was with him, the stronger those feelings grew.

Winnie's face lit up when she saw Colt. "You're alive."

"Yes, thanks to Ellie." He slanted a look at her before stooping by Winnie. "Are you doing okay?"

"Now I am. What happened?"

As Colt told his grandmother, her face hardened more and more into a scowl.

"I hope he's trapped in the avalanche," Winnie blurted out at the end. "Evil begets evil."

One of Colt's eyebrows lifted. "No forgiveness for the man?"

Winnie pursed her mouth. "I'm working on it, but his actions are making it very hard. It's one thing to go after me, but he was trying to kill you. He needs to be stopped, and if the avalanche did it, so be it."

Ellie sat, her legs trembling from exhaustion. "We need to come up with a plan to get out of here. Colt, you said there's only one way into this cave. You've explored this place completely?"

"There's another way in that is blocked on the other side. This system goes through the mountain we are on."

"What do you mean by blocked?"

"Years ago there was a rockslide. There's an opening, but it isn't big. I'm not sure I can fit through it. For all I know the rocks may have shifted and closed it completely off."

"Or opened it up some more. Would the assailant know about the back way into this cave?" Ellie slid her glance to Winnie, who pulled the blanket around herself, her lips quivering.

"Unless you're really familiar with the area, you wouldn't know about it. Like I said, this is Winfield property."

"Let's hope he isn't because I don't think we can wait around to see if anyone finds us and digs us out."

"Agreed."

"Winnie, if Colt and I help you, do you think you can make it through the cave to the other side?"

She lifted her chin. "Don't you two worry about me. I'll do what I have to. If I can't make it, you can leave me and come back to get me after you find a way out."

"We can't leave you alone." Colt wrapped his arms around his grandmother.

"I'm not afraid. The Lord will be with me."

"It may not be an issue if I can carry you."

Ellie gathered up all the backpacks and supplies and led the way Colt told her to go while he carried his grandmother in his arms. Dripping water and their breathing were the only sounds in the cavern. The chill burrowed into Ellie's bones the deeper they went into the heart of the mountain.

"How long ago were you last here?" Ellie asked as the passage became narrower and shorter.

"At least ten years ago."

Ellie glanced back at Colt. Winnie's head was cushioned against his shoulder, her eyes closed. "Was there any crawling involved?"

He nodded. "Come to think of it, the cave gets tight in one area."

When Ellie reached a fork in the cave system, she stopped. "Which way?"

Colt shut his eyes, his forehead wrinkled. "I think to the right. This probably isn't the time to tell you I'm lousy with telling you the difference in right or left."

"There's no good time to tell me that," she said. "I could go a ways and see what I find."

"No, we'll stay together. If it's the way, you'd have to track back." Colt shifted Winnie some in his embrace and winced.

"Are you all right?"

"I hurt my arm when the whole mountain came down on me."

"Just your arm? Let's take a rest, eat something and drink some water."

"We should keep going."

"Our bodies need the rest, food and water." Ellie plopped the backpacks down on the stone floor and helped Colt lower his grandmother onto a blanket.

"You two don't have to stop for me," Winnie murmured, pain etched into her features.

"We're stopping for all of us." Ellie delved into her backpack and found the granola bars and a bottle of water. "It may be freezing, but we still have to keep ourselves hydrated."

"Just a short break." Colt removed his gloves and rubbed his left arm.

Shivering, Winnie took the first sip of water then passed it to Ellie. When she gave it to Colt, the touch of his cold fingers against hers fastened her attention on him. In the dim lighting his light blue eyes looked dark. Shadows played across his strong jaw. But the sear of his gaze warmed her as though she sat in front of a flaming blaze.

"I wonder if the cabin caught fire." Colt bit into his granola bar.

"If it did, maybe someone will see the smoke and investigate. They might be concerned about a forest fire." Winnie began unlacing the shoe she had put back on when they'd started the journey through the cave.

"Maybe, but we're isolated up here and the conditions down the mountain might be worse than up here." He popped the last bite into his mouth.

Winnie took off her boot to reveal a swollen ankle, worse than before. "I can't wear this anymore. It's killing my foot. Oh, dear, that was a poor choice of words."

"But true. I've had a sprained ankle, and it does hurt to wear close-fitting shoes." Ellie unwound her scarf and wrapped it around Winnie's foot.

"I can't take your scarf. You need it."

"Nonsense, you need it more than me. One layer of socks isn't warm enough. I find feet, head and hands get cold faster than other parts of your body. If you keep them covered it helps you feel warmer."

Winnie smiled, but the gesture didn't stay on

her face more than a second. "I can hardly keep my eyes open."

"Then keep them closed. I'm carrying you, anyway." Colt rose. "Ready."

"Are you sure?" Ellie mouthed the question to Colt, touching his hurt arm.

He nodded.

"If the cabin is gone, I won't get to see what you brought in the sack for me and Ellie." Winnie snuggled close to Colt's body.

"What if it isn't burned down?"

Ellie replied, "I think you should tell us, anyway. Don't you, Winnie?"

"Yes."

He exaggerated a sigh, but the corners of his mouth quirked up, his left dimple appearing in his cheek. "Doug carved a German shepherd like Lady for me to give to you, Winnie, and I found my mom's locket in my belongings in the closet when I put my speargun back." His gaze fastened onto Ellie. "I hope you'll accept it."

Her throat closed, emotions she couldn't express rushing to the surface. "I shouldn't. It's your mother's."

"She'd want you to have it. You've gone above and beyond your duties as a bodyguard."

"I totally agree, Colt," Winnie said. "I hope you'll accept it, Ellie, if it didn't burn."

"I'd be honored," she murmured.

Colt cleared his throat. "We'd better get going."

As Ellie continued their trek, the ceiling dropped more until Colt had to bend over while carrying his grandmother through the passage. When Ellie peered at the pair, she noticed Colt's back kept scraping the roof of the cave. Strain marked his features as he struggled to stay on his feet with Winnie in his arms. Ellie rounded a corner in the passageway and came to a stop.

"Does this look familiar, because if it doesn't maybe we should try the other path?" Ellie waved her hand ahead of them at a tunnel about four feet wide and three feet tall.

Colt paused behind her and put his grandmother on the floor. "Yes. I'd forgotten I had to crawl part of the way toward the end. I've been in a lot of caves through the years. They kind of all run together."

"Let me wait here while you two check it out," Winnie said. "I'll be fine. I can catch a catnap. If it turns out to be a way out, you can come back for me. If it doesn't, then we don't have to try and get me through there."

"I don't want to leave—"

"Ellie, we're trapped in a cave with a mound of snow standing between us and the person after me. I think I'll be perfectly safe here by myself."

"I'll go alone, and if it's the way out, I'll come

back and get both of you." Colt moved toward the narrow passageway. "Rest, Winnie. It's not far from here so I shouldn't be gone long."

Ellie helped make Winnie more comfortable. Since this ordeal had started, she had appeared to age a couple of years. Ellie was concerned about her. Winnie had been working so hard the past year on the Endless Youth products and then to have to run for her life… It might be too much for even a tough lady like her.

Although her eyes were closed, Winnie huddled in the blanket up against Ellie and said, "Since this began I've been thanking God for sending you to me. Now I'm thanking you for staying for Christmas. I doubt it's your idea of how to celebrate Christmas, but I'm mighty grateful you're here, and if I'm not mistaken, so is my grandson."

"Here we are trapped in a cave and you're matchmaking."

"You can't blame a grandmother for trying. I've got a captive audience," Winnie said with a chuckle, some of her fight surfacing.

"I like Colt." *A lot.*

"What I've seen makes me think it's more than just like. Or is that wishful thinking on my part?"

Ellie opened her mouth to say, "Yes," but the word wouldn't come out because it wasn't the truth. "No, there is more, but Winnie, I just don't see how..." She didn't know how to explain her mixed-up feelings even to herself, let alone someone else.

"I know you both have separate lives, but even when two people live in the same town and their lives mesh together, a relationship can be hard. Colt needs someone like you in his life."

"You're right about the hurdles between us."

"Thomas and I had hurdles, too, but we overcame them. He'd just divorced his wife a couple of months before we started dating, but we'd known each other and worked together for several years. People took our openly dating as a sign we'd been having an affair while he was married, especially his ex-wife. She made our lives unbearable for a while, then thankfully she decided to move away and we began to have a normal relationship. Thomas was a wonderful stepfather to my son. In fact, he adopted him when we got married."

Marrying. Having a relationship. Where does that fit in my life? She'd spent her years just trying to survive and have a life with meaning. Her work and faith had given her that. But if she gave in to her feelings concerning Colt, everything would change. So much of her life had been one change after another and she had needed some stability, which her vision for her life had given her—until now.

The passageway narrowed even more. Colt flattened himself and pulled his body through the stone-cold corridor. Although pain stabbed his left bicep, he kept going because a freezing wind whipped by him, indicating there was a way out of the cave up ahead. Reaching forward to grasp something to help him slither through the tunnel, he clutched air. Nothing. He focused the small flashlight on the spot in front of him and saw a drop-off.

Dragging himself to the edge of the opening of the passageway, he stared down at a black hole where the floor of the cavern should be. Across from him, not thirty feet away, light streamed into the darkness. He swung his flashlight toward the area and saw the rocks he remembered piled up where the second cave entrance used to be.

So close with a thirty-foot gap between him and freedom.

"What's keeping Colt? He should have been back by now." Winnie's teeth chattered.

Ellie rubbed her gloved hands up and down Winnie's arms. "It might have been farther than he thought. It hasn't been that long." She infused an upbeat tone into her voice because she knew the cold was getting to Winnie. "Tell me some more about your marriage to Thomas. It sounds like you two were very happy."

"Don't get me wrong. We had our problems, especially concerning Colt's father, but we always managed to work them out. As long as we had each other, we felt we could deal with anything."

"That's nice. No wonder you're a romantic at heart."

"Me? What gave you that idea?"

"Oh, the flowers in your house, a tradition your husband started and you continued. The way you talk about Thomas. But mostly some of the products your company sells with names like Only Her and Only Him."

"You aren't a romantic?"

"Never had time for romance in my life."

"Why not?"

Ellie ended up telling a second person about her childhood. "What is it about a Winfield demanding to know stuff I've never shared with others?"

"It's our charm." Winnie grinned, a sparkle in her eyes for the first time since they'd started on this trek hours ago. "That and we care. People sense that about us. Hard to resist."

"That could be it."

A sound behind Ellie turned her in the direction of the tunnel. Colt crawled out of the hole, his features set in grim determination.

"Something wrong?" she asked.

He shook his head. "The tunnel is narrower than I remember, but if I can get through, you two can. Anyone larger than me won't, though. When I reached the other end, there is a sheer drop-off at the opening that wasn't there before, but the hole in the cavern is only four feet deep. I'll be able to lower myself to the floor and make my way to the entrance. It's still partially blocked. I may have to move a few rocks, but I'll be able to get through the hole."

"So bring back some skinny people to help us," Ellie said.

He laughed, then gathered what he was going to take with him—snowshoes, gun, tinted goggles. "I'll keep that in mind. Stay here. It's warmer in this cavern than the other one."

At the entrance to the tunnel, Ellie placed her hand on his arm.

He turned toward her.

"Keep safe. If an avalanche happened once, it can again."

His smile began as a twinkle in his eyes and spread to transform his earlier serious expression. "I like this role of knight in shining armor."

"Well, in that case, here's a token of my appreciation." She produced his scarf he'd left on the floor and put it around his neck. "It's cold out there."

"It's cold in here."

"True, but not as much wind." Her gaze linked with his. "I mean it. Don't take any unnecessary risks."

"Then it's okay to take necessary risks?"

"I'll be praying."

"Me, too, Colt," Winnie said from where she was sitting against the wall of the cave.

Colt stepped around Ellie, made his way to his grandmother, whispered something to her then kissed her on the head.

When he returned to Ellie, he caught her hands and brought them up between them, inching toward her until they touched. "I probably won't be back for a while."

"I know."

He leaned down and claimed her mouth in a kiss that rocked Ellie to her core, mocking her intention of keeping herself apart from him. It was so hard when he was storming every defense she put up to keep people away.

He pulled back, stared at her for a long moment then ducked down and disappeared into the tunnel. She watched him crawl toward the exit, his light fading. *What if I never see him again?* Her heart lurched at that thought.

Lord, keep him safe. Please. You're in control.

Although the temptation was great to check out the front of the cave and the cabin, Colt couldn't. That would eat into time he didn't have if he was going to get help back up the mountain before dark. He didn't know how long Winnie could last in this freezing weather. She had never tolerated the cold like he and his granddad had.

When he wiggled himself through the opening in the cave, he emerged into more falling snow, but at least it wasn't coming down too hard. Actually the snow could work to his advantage by covering his tracks if the assailant was still alive and out there waiting.

The scent of smoke hovered in the air. He looked in the direction of the cabin but couldn't see any flames. A dense cloud cover hung low over the area.

In his mind he plotted the trail he would take to the estate. Once there, he could use the phone and call for help. Then he and Doug could start up the mountain even before a rescue team could form and make it up to the cave.

Hours later, only a short distance from the

house, Colt pushed himself faster. It would be dark before he could get back up the mountain if he didn't move more quickly. Although his legs shook with fatigue, he put one foot in front of the other, sometimes dragging himself out of a hole when he sank too far into the snow. But once he made it over the last ridge he would nearly be home. That thought urged him to pick up speed yet again.

When he put his foot down in front of him, the snow gave away, sending him tumbling down the incline. When he rolled to the bottom, he crashed into a pine tree, knocking the breath from him. Snow crusted him from head to foot. He wiped it away from his goggles and saw two snow boots planted apart. His gaze traveled upward past two legs and a heavy coat to a face covered in a white ski mask.

"Do you think Colt is all right? What if the bad guy didn't get caught in the avalanche and was waiting for him? I can't lose my grandson." Winnie took a sip from the bottle of water then passed it to Ellie.

"Colt can take care of himself." She prayed she was right.

"I know. I shouldn't worry. It does no good but get me upset."

"In a perfect world we wouldn't worry." Ellie worried, too. So many things could go wrong.

"We're safe in here while he's—"

A roar split the air, sending goose bumps flashing up Ellie's body.

Winnie's eyes grew round and huge. "That's—that's a..." She gulped, the color washing from her face.

"A bear. Nearby."

"In this cave!" Winnie sat up straight, the blanket falling away from her. "What's it doing in here?"

"It's a cave and wintertime. Hibernating?" Ellie quickly gathered up all their belongings and stuffed them into one of the backpacks.

"What do we do?" Winnie asked at the same time another deep growl echoed through the cave.

"Get out of here."

"How? It sounds like it's coming down the passageway we used."

"We're going through the tunnel. Chances are it can't get through there. It's probably still fat since it's only December." Ellie felt for her gun at her hip. "If I have to, I will shoot it. Do you think you can crawl through the tunnel?"

"If I have to, I will."

Ellie helped Winnie to her feet, then supported most of her weight as the woman hopped toward the escape route. "You go first. I'm going in backward so if the bear follows, I can take care of it. From what Colt said, there is no room to turn around. Okay?"

Taking one of the flashlights, Winnie knelt before the entrance and began crawling forward. Ellie backed into the tunnel, pulling the backpack after her. Through the opening she glimpsed a brown bear loping into the area where they had been, sniffing the air. It released another roar, lumbered to the hole and stuck its head inside.

Colt started to spring up when a shovel crashed down on top of him, glancing off his head and striking his shoulder. His ears rang. The whole world spun for a few seconds. The man lifted the weapon again. Colt dropped back to the ground and rolled hard into the man. The action sent a wave of dizziness through Colt, but toppled his assailant to the snow.

Facedown, Colt fumbled in his coat pocket for his gun, fighting the whirling sensation attacking his mind. Before he could pull it out, his attacker whacked the shovel across his back. Again, pain shot through his body. Someone yelled right before blackness swallowed him up.

"That's the bear!" Winnie said behind Ellie in the tunnel.

"A big one thankfully. I don't think it can get

in here. Keep moving as fast as you can just in case."

Keeping her eye on the bear and her gun aimed at it, Ellie listened to Winnie's struggles as she made her way. Ellie didn't want to go any farther until she knew what the bear was going to do. Even if the animal tried to fit into the narrow passage, it wouldn't be able to do much. She calmed her speeding heartbeat.

Wiping first one sweating hand then the other against her coat, she locked gazes with the beast, giving it the most intimidating glare she could muster. "I'm not letting you pass. Don't make me hurt you." A fierce strength coated each word.

The bear released another growl. Its long teeth ridiculed her statements. The animal pushed forward a few inches but didn't go any farther because the walls sloped inward at that point. Finally it gave one last glower then backed out of the entrance into the tunnel.

"There's a really narrow part," Winnie said behind her.

When the bear disappeared from her view, Ellie scooted backward toward the other end. Sounds of the animal drifted to her, but it hadn't returned to the tunnel. A chill pervaded the passage, especially the closer she came to the exit. The thought that it was even colder than where they had been worried Ellie. Winnie needed medical attention and warmth. Ellie couldn't give her either.

"Colt." A familiar male voice filtered into Colt's pain-riddled mind.

The first sensation Colt experienced besides the drumming throb against his skull was the chill penetrating through his clothing. He opened his eyes to find someone kneeling next to him. With his cheek pressed against the snow, frigid, biting, Colt fought the urge to surrender again to the darkness.

"Colt, I was checking the grounds when I heard a noise and looked up the rise. I saw someone attacking you."

Relief that it was Doug pushed Colt to keep himself as alert as possible. Winnie and Ellie were depending on him. Moaning, he lifted his head and regretted it instantly. The world tilted before him. He closed his eyes, but it still swirled. He didn't have time for this. He forced down the nausea churning his stomach and slowly he rolled to face upward. Snow-flakes pelted him, but the storm had lessened. Which meant whoever attacked him could possibly find the other entrance into the cave because his footprints weren't totally covered by the falling snow.

"Winnie and Ellie are trapped in the cave system near the cabin, the one I told you about." Somehow he strung together a sentence that made sense.

Doug looked up at the mountain. "That's the way your attacker fled."

Colt struggled to prop himself up on his elbows, searching for the tracks the man made. If he moved slowly, the world didn't spin too much. "I was coming to the house to call for help. There was an avalanche and it blocked the front of the cave. I used the back way in on the other side of the mountain. It's blocked, but I managed to remove a few rocks and wiggle out of the opening."

"Let's get you to the house and call 911, then I'll go up there."

"No, you go back. We're almost into cell range. Alert the sheriff then follow my tracks. I have to go. If that man finds Winnie and Ellie, he'll kill them. He tried to burn the cabin down."

"But wasn't Mary Ann Witlock the one threatening Winnie?"

"Maybe this guy was helping her."

Taking it slow, Colt tucked his legs under him then pushed himself to stand. Doug hurried to assist him. Colt's body protested with his every move, but he managed to remain upright. Then he put one foot in front of the other and started up the mountain, following his assailant's tracks.

He glanced back at Doug and the man was almost to the fence line at the estate. Help wouldn't be too far behind, but Colt had to quicken his pace if he was going to stop the attacker from harming Winnie and Ellie.

I need Your help, Lord. I can't do this without You. Anything is possible with You.

While Winnie stayed on the ledge at the tunnel, Ellie lowered herself over the cave shelf, clinging to a protruding rock. When her feet touched the floor, she let go of the stone, then positioned herself near the wall.

"Okay, Winnie. I'm going to guide you down and hold you so you don't put any weight on your bad foot."

"I still hear the bear. Do you think it can get through that tunnel?"

"No. It's angry we got away. Come on. We'll find a place to settle down and wait for Colt where we can also keep an eye on the tunnel."

After Winnie made it to the floor of the cavern, Ellie swung her light around to find the best place to wait. Puddles of icy water littered the area. Wind blew through the opening.

"The good news is that the water isn't totally frozen so the temperature isn't much below freezing."

Winnie snorted. "Tell that to my body."

Ellie pointed to a place a few feet away. "It's dry there and it looks like it'll shelter us from the wind. And I can see the tunnel."

Shielded from the wind slipping through the opening, Ellie cocooned Winnie in as much warmth as possible. She even used the backpack for her to sit on. "There. Now it's just a matter of a couple of hours. Everything will be over."

"No, it won't. We don't know who is after me. Who might have worked with Mary Ann?"

"I know we looked into her background and no one stood out. She didn't have a boyfriend, and the couple of members of her family who worked for Glamour Sensations didn't have much to do with her."

"One of the reasons I didn't pick her to be the spokesperson for Endless Youth was the way she always came across as though she were ten or fifteen years older than she was. An old soul but not in a good way. Weary. Unhappy. That wasn't the image I wanted to project for this line. Christy is the opposite of that. Young at heart although she is thirty-two. I didn't want a woman who was too young, but I wanted one who had an exuberance in spirit about her. I was so happy when Christy started dating Peter.

She'd been engaged once before, and he was killed in a motorcycle accident." Winnie hugged her arms against her chest.

Ellie needed to keep her talking about anything but the situation they were in. "I understand that Christy became engaged to Peter right after you chose her as the spokesperson. Will that interfere in your advertising plans for the product?"

"No, Peter assured me he would do whatever Christy needed. He's been a great support for her. I was surprised at how fast he moved. They'd only been dating a couple of months. I think secretly—although he would never admit it—that he was afraid once the world saw her another man would snatch her right up. Men and claiming their territory." Winnie chuckled. "But I can't complain. Thomas was just like Peter. We only dated a few months, too. Of course, we worked together for a while before that."

"They know a good woman when they see her," Ellie said over the howl of the wind, its force increasing through the cave.

"Yes, and I'm hoping my grandson follows in his granddad's footsteps."

Even in the shadows created by the dim light, Ellie could see Winnie's gleaming eyes. "I have a very persuasive boss who has tried her best to fix me up with a couple of men she knows in Dallas. So far I've not succumbed to her tactics."

"Colt needs someone like you."

"I refuse to say anything to that. I'm sure there is a better subject than my love life."

Winnie's forehead crinkled. "You know, I've been thinking. Not many people knew we were coming up here. We really didn't make the final decision until we talked with the sheriff yesterday. Remember?"

"Yes. We were having a late breakfast. But only Linda was in the room besides the sheriff and us."

Winnie gasped. "It couldn't be Linda, Doug or the sheriff."

A sound above Winnie drew Ellie's gaze. On top of the ledge stood a man dressed in white wearing a white ski mask with a gun aimed at Winnie.

Chapter Twelve

"Who are you?" Ellie asked the man on the ledge.

He cackled. "I'm not telling you. You two can die wondering who I am, especially after all the trouble you've put me through today."

"Why me?" Winnie lifted her face toward her assailant. "What have I done to you?"

"You continually have ruined my life," he said in a voice roughened as if he disguised it.

"I couldn't have. I haven't done that to anyone. I would know about it."

"Well, obviously you don't," the man shouted, his gun wavering as anger poured off him.

Ellie glanced at her gun lying on the ground next to her. She gauged her chances of grabbing it and getting a shot off before he did.

"Don't think about it. I'd have Winnie dead before you could aim the gun."

The voice, although muffled by the ski mask some, sounded familiar to Ellie. She'd heard him before—recently. Could it be Doug? The sheriff?

"Why me?" Winnie asked the gunman. "Don't you want me to know why you're killing me? What satisfaction can you have in that if I don't know why, especially if I wronged you as you say?" A mocking tone inched into Winnie's voice.

Ellie needed to keep the man talking. "As far as we know you're a maniac who belongs in a mental—"

His harsh laugh cut off the rest of her sentence. "Colt isn't coming to your rescue. I left him for dead and followed his trail to you two. How accommodating he was to show me where you all were."

No, Colt can't be dead. He's psyching me out. Trying to rattle me.

"I guess you should know why, Winnie." He said her name slowly, bitterness dripping from it. "You stole my father from my mother."

Winnie gasped.

"If you hadn't come along, my parents would have gotten back together. I would have had a father who would acknowledge me. Instead, he wouldn't have anything to do with me. You poisoned him. You kept him from me."

"Thomas didn't have a child. Thomas couldn't have one."

"Liar!"

"The doctors told Thomas it was impossible, and we never could have children." The pain in Winnie's voice was reflected in her expression, too.

"I am Thomas Winfield's son. My mama showed me my birth certificate. It was right there on the paper. There wasn't a day that went by that I wasn't reminded I wasn't good enough to be a Winfield. He discarded my mother and me like we were trash."

"Are you talking about Clare, Thomas's first wife?"

"Yes. He decided to divorce her for you."

"No, he didn't. We didn't start dating until after the divorce."

"That's not what my mama told me. Why in the world would I believe you? My father wasn't the only one you took away from me. Everything I wanted you came after. Well, not anymore. I'm putting an end to you." He lowered the gun a few inches and pointed it right at Winnie's heart.

Ellie yanked Winnie toward her at the same time a shot rang out in the cave. Snatching her weapon from the floor, she raised it toward their attacker while putting herself in between

Winnie and the man. But Ellie didn't get off a shot. Instead, his arm fell to his side, the gun dropping from his fingers. It bounced on the stone surface, going off, the bullet lodging in the wall. Blood spread outward on the white jacket he wore as he crumbled to the ground.

As Ellie scrambled up, she glimpsed Colt diving through the hole and springing to his feet, his gun pointed at their assailant.

"Ellie, Winnie, are you two all right?"

"Yes," they both answered at the same time.

Ellie swiveled toward Winnie. "Are you really okay?"

She nodded. "At least I'm not cold anymore. Fear will do that to you."

Ellie headed up the sloping side to the ledge above Winnie and joined Colt as he knelt next to the gunman. He removed the man's goggles then his white ski mask to reveal Peter Tyler, blinking his eyes at the light she shone on his face.

Ellie stared at the glittering Christmas tree in the living room at Winnie's house. Although it was Christmas Day, there had been nothing calm and peaceful so far. Winnie had spent time with Christy, consoling her over her fiancé. Harold and Colt had been behind closed doors a good part of the morning, then Colt insisted

Winnie rest before the sheriff came this afternoon. He had an update on what Peter Tyler had said after he came out of surgery to repair his shoulder where Colt had shot him. Colt and Doug had gone up to the cabin to see what was left of the place. Colt had wanted her to come, but she'd felt she needed to stay with Winnie. After what had occurred with Mary Ann, she wasn't quite ready to relinquish her bodyguard duties with Winnie until she had reassurances from the sheriff.

Then she would return to Dallas. And try to put her life back together. She finally could admit to herself that she loved Colt, but how could she really be sure? Even if she was, that didn't mean he cared about her or that they should be together. He lived on a research vessel in the middle of the ocean. She could never imagine herself living like that.

When the doorbell rang, she hurried across the foyer to answer it. Stepping to the side, she let the sheriff into the house. "I hope you're here to tell us good news."

"Yes," he said as Winnie descended the stairs and Colt came from the kitchen.

"Would you like anything to drink? We have some cookies, too." Winnie gestured toward the living room.

"Nope. Just as soon as we talk, I'm heading

home. My son and grandchildren are there waiting for me so they can open presents. I haven't quite had a Christmas like this year in—well, never." Sheriff Quinn stood in front of the fireplace, warming himself. "I came right from the hospital after interviewing Peter. I laid it on the line. We have him dead to rights on three counts of attempted murder, arson and a number of other charges. I told him the judge would look kindly toward him if we didn't have to drag this out in a lengthy trial. He told me what happened."

Winnie frowned. "What was his involvement with Mary Ann?"

Colt hung back by the entrance into the living room, leaning against the wall, his arms folded over his chest. Ellie glanced toward him, but his expression was unreadable, his gaze fixed on his grandmother.

"He encouraged her to act on her feelings and gave her suggestions. When she was his patient, they got acquainted. He listened to her when she ranted about not getting the spokesperson job, then began planting seeds in her mind about how she had not been treated fairly. The threatening letters were Mary Ann's doing and the stink bombs at the Christmas Gala. He helped her kidnap the dogs because he told her that she could get some good money for them and get back at Winnie."

"Your lead didn't pan out about the dogs. Does he know where they are?" Colt asked, coming farther into the room and sitting next to Winnie.

"Yes, because he connected her with the person who took them to sell in Denver. The police there are paying that gentleman a visit today before he gets rid of them. You should have your dogs home by tomorrow."

"Unless someone bought them for a Christmas gift." Exhaustion still clung to Winnie's face, especially her eyes.

"Then we'll track each purchase."

"Winnie, they're alive. That's good news." Colt took her hand in his.

"So Peter Tyler was responsible in part about the dogs. How about the car left in the middle of the road the night of the Christmas tree lighting?" she asked.

"That was him. He didn't care whether you went off the cliff like Thomas or got upset by the similarities between the two events."

Winnie sat forward. "Wait. He didn't have anything to do with Thomas's accident, did he?"

"No, at least that's what he said, and all the evidence still points to an accident, Winnie. He wasn't even living here at that time.

He moved back not long after he saw in the newspaper about Thomas dying. His mother had passed away a few months before your husband. According to Peter, she was still broken-hearted after all the years they were divorced. She fed Peter a lot of garbage about you coming between her and Thomas. I told him that wasn't the case. You two worked in the lab together, but so did my mother and she said it was hogwash what Thomas's ex-wife was saying."

Winnie smiled, and even her eyes sparkled with the gesture. "Your mom is a good friend."

"She sends her regards from sunny Florida. I can't get her back here in the winter. Too cold."

Winnie laughed. "I heartily agree with her. I may go visit her and warm these cold bones."

"We didn't make the final decision to go to the cabin until you told us it was safe. How did Peter know we were there?" Ellie asked Sheriff Quinn.

"He knew there was a chance, based on the talk the night before. He planned ahead, staying in a small cabin not far from you on the Henderson property. Then he came back to watch and see if you went." The sheriff held his hands out over the fire and rubbed them together.

Ellie liked seeing Winnie's smile and hearing her laugh. The past weeks' ordeal had taken a toll on the woman. After the doctor at the house had checked out Winnie, she'd slept for twelve hours last night. Winnie had insisted Colt go to the hospital and have some X-rays on his arm. Ellie had taken him but little was said. In fact, Colt dozed on the trip to the hospital where the doctor told him he would be sore for a while, but he hadn't fractured his arm. Colt had also suffered a mild concussion, but he'd refused to stay overnight.

"Winnie, you could always return with me to the *Kaleidoscope*. We're in warm waters. In the South Pacific, it's summer right now."

"Not if I have to live on a boat."

Colt smiled. "It's a ship."

"Not big enough for me. You know I can't swim. You didn't get the swimming gene from me."

"Speaking of genes. Is Peter my uncle?"

Winnie shuddered. "Good grief, no. I don't know who his father is, but Thomas was sterile. For some reason she used Thomas to blame all her woes on. I guess that was easier for her than changing."

"I'm heading home to salvage a little bit of Christmas with my family." The sheriff crossed the room to the foyer, and Colt walked with him to the front door.

Winnie pinned Ellie with an assessing look.

"You've been quiet. I imagine you're glad this is over with about as much as I am."

"I'm usually like this when a job is finished. It takes me days to come down from the stress. How's Christy? She looked much better after she talked with you this morning."

"At first she wanted to step down from being the spokesperson for Endless Youth, but I talked her out of that. I told her she's not responsible for other people's actions. She isn't to blame for Peter or Mary Ann. Christy told me she talked with Peter before he went into surgery. What sent Peter over the edge was that Christy got the job that would demand a lot of her time—time away from him. He came to Bakersville after years of being told I was the one who caused all the trouble for him and his mother. He struggled to make it through school and has a huge debt from college loans he's still paying back. He saw the money he thought he should rightly have as Thomas's only living son. It festered inside him. The trigger was Christy getting the job and getting all the attention. But it was Peter's problem, not hers."

"Can you forgive Peter for what he did?"

"Probably when I recover from the effects of yesterday. Hanging on to the anger will only hurt me in the long run. Look what happened to Peter and his mother when they held on to their anger."

Listening to Winnie's reasonable explanation of why she would forgive Peter made Ellie think about her mother. She hadn't talked to her in years, and that had always bothered her. Maybe she should call her tonight and wish her a merry Christmas.

Colt reentered the living room. "I'm glad this is all wrapped up. I got a message from the *Kaleidoscope*. Doug gave it to me this morning. I'm needed back there to finish up a study we've been running on the seal population in the area where we're anchored."

"When?" Winnie rose.

"Day after tomorrow. I want to make sure you're all right and things are really settled after what's happened."

"At least we have a little more time together. I think I'll take my second nap today. See you two at dinner."

After Winnie left, Colt took the couch across from Ellie. He stared at the fire for a long moment before looking at her. "One thing my grandmother isn't is subtle. For being tired, she can move awfully fast."

"I think she's still trying to process it all. Having not just one but two people angry with you to the point they wanted to harm you is hard on even the toughest person. Imagine Peter's mother lying to him for all those years."

"It just makes me realize how fortunate I've been to have Winnie and my granddad to raise me."

"I'm going to call my mother tonight. It's about time I did. I don't expect warm fuzzies, but I need to take the first step to try and mend our relationship. She's all the family I have. I see the relationship you have with Winnie, and although we'll probably never have that kind, we can at least have a civil one."

"You get a chance to do that. I don't have that. My father is dead."

"You can forgive him in your heart. That's what is important."

"You're right." Colt stood and bridged the distance between them. "Speaking of relationships, what are we going to do about us?"

"Nothing."

He clasped her hands and hauled her up against him. "You can't deny we have a connection."

"No, I can't. But this isn't real. This whole situation heightened all our senses. I've seen it before with others and their relationships didn't last. You and I live very differently. I couldn't live on a research vessel even if it's classified a ship. I need space. I would go crazy. How could a relationship last with you in the Pacific Ocean and me flying all over the world for my job? I think we should cut our losses and go our separate ways."

"How do you feel about me? Forget about what you just said. All the logical, rational reasons we shouldn't be together." He placed his hand over her heart. "How do you feel in there?"

"I love you, but it isn't enough. A lasting relationship is much more than love. We haven't had any time to think about our feelings. We've been on a roller-coaster ride since you arrived."

He framed her face. "I love you, Ellie. I don't want to let you go. I realized that when I was trying to get back to you and Winnie in the cave. I thought I was going to lose you when I saw Peter pointing the gun at you."

His declaration made her hesitate, her resolve wavering. Finally she murmured, "Someone has to be the logical, rational one. I guess I'm that one. I need time to figure out what I want. You need time. You have a job that needs you right now and so do I."

He bent toward her and kissed her. All the sensations he could produce in her flooded her, making her want to take a risk. When he pulled back, sanity returned to Ellie.

"Why not give the *Kaleidoscope* a chance? You might like it."

She shook her head.

"No, I'm leaving tomorrow morning to return to Dallas. Maybe sometime in the future we'll meet again under less stressful circumstances."

He released a long breath. "You're right. These past few weeks have been unreal. Reality is our everyday lives. Will you promise me one thing?"

"Maybe."

He chuckled. "Why am I not surprised you said that? Where's the trust?"

"That's just the point. I don't trust easily and these new feelings could all vanish with time."

"Winnie will be having an Endless Youth gala to launch the new line on Valentine's Day. In spite of what happened the last time, she'll be having it at the same hotel that evening. Come back. Meet me there if you think we have a chance at what we started here. That's seven weeks away."

"I promise I'll think long and hard on it."

"You do that," he said. "And I hope I'll see you then."

Colt stood at the double doors into the hotel ballroom on Valentine's Day. The event was in full swing. Laughter floated to him. A sense of celebration dominated the atmosphere of the Endless Youth gala. The music, soft and romantic, filled the room. Couples, dressed in tuxedos and gowns, whirled around the dance floor to the strains of a waltz.

None of the gaiety meant anything to him.

The ball was halfway over. Ellie wasn't here. She wasn't coming.

"Colt, why aren't you dancing?"

He forced a smile for his grandmother, but inside his heart was breaking. "You sent Ellie the invitation?"

"For the third time, yes, and I know she received it."

"I gave her the space she wanted."

"Then you've done what you can. Have faith in what you feel, what you two shared at Christmas. I saw how she felt about you. Give her time to work it out. Why don't you dance with your favorite grandmother?"

"You're my *only* grandmother."

"True."

"You know dancing isn't my thing. Harold is so much better than me, and he is your date for tonight."

"Just because Harold and I are dating doesn't mean I should neglect my grandson." She laughed, a sound Colt loved to hear from his grandmother. "I can't believe I'm dating again. I thought that would never happen after Thomas."

"Why not? You're seventy-three years *young*."

"You're right." Winnie held her hand out to Colt.

He threw a last glance over his shoulder at the hotel lobby. No Ellie. After three days on the *Kaleidoscope* he'd known what he'd felt for her was the marrying kind of love. There was no thrill and excitement in his job. He wanted to share his life with Ellie. He'd completed his research project and resigned. It was time for him to put down roots. Alone, if not with Ellie.

He whisked his grandmother out onto the dance floor and somehow managed to sweep Winnie around the ballroom to some love song without stepping on her foot or stumbling.

Then he saw her, dressed in a long red gown, across the room in the entrance to the ballroom. Ellie had come. He came to a standstill. Their gazes linked together, and his heart began pounding against his chest.

"Go to her," Winnie whispered, backing away from him.

Colt headed toward Ellie at the same time she did. They met on the edge of the dance floor. He was sure he had some silly grin on his face, but Ellie's smile encompassed her whole face in radiance.

"You look beautiful. Want to dance?" He offered her his hand.

She clasped it and came effortlessly into his embrace. The feel of her against him felt so right.

"I'm sorry I was late. My flight was delayed then we had to change planes and—"

He stopped her words with a kiss. When he drew back and began to move about the floor, he said, "You're here. That's all that's important."

They flowed as one through the crowd of dancers. All he could do was stare at her. He never wanted to take his eyes off her again.

"Seven weeks was too long to be apart. When I returned to the *Kaleidoscope,* my life wasn't the same. I wanted different things. I love you, Ellie."

"The same for me. I went back to Dallas. I even went on an assignment in Rome. I love Rome. I stayed a few days after my job was finished, but Rome wasn't the same without you. I tried to talk myself out of my feelings, but I couldn't, not in seven weeks. That's when I knew I had to see you again. Be with you."

The music stopped. Colt grabbed her hand and hurried off the dance floor out into the lobby. He found a private alcove and pulled her back into his arms.

"I want to be with you, too," he said.

"Our jobs—"

He put two fingers over her lips, the feel of them against his skin everything he remembered. Warm. Soft. Her. "I resigned from the *Kaleidoscope*. I'm slowly going to take over for Winnie. She wants to retire completely in a year or so. She says she's ready to lie around and eat bonbons."

Ellie laughed. "That'll be the day. She'll hole herself in her lab in the basement and create some other sensational product."

"As the soon-to-be CEO of Glamour Sensations, I'm hoping she will. What would you say if we hired you as the head of our security? The company is growing. I need someone with more experience than our current guy. Security will become more important than ever before. And there will still be some travel involved so you won't always be confined to here."

She snuggled closer. "I like being confined to here if you're here, too."

"Right by your side. I hope as your husband." Then he kissed her with every emotion he'd held in check for the past seven weeks without her.

"I think I can accommodate that."

* * * * *

Dear Reader,

Christmas Stalking is the fourth in my Guardians, Inc. series, where the women and men are both equally strong characters who know how to deal with dangerous situations. I've had readers write to me about how much they enjoy seeing a woman play a tough role and still be soft and vulnerable enough to fall in love. I have two more books coming in this series for Love Inspired Suspense. Look for them in the future.

I love hearing from readers. You can contact me at margaretdaley@gmail.com or at P.O. Box 2074, Tulsa, OK 74101. You can also learn more about my books at www.margaretdaley.com. I have a newsletter that you can sign up for on my website.

Best wishes,

Margaret Daley

Questions for Discussion

1. Trust is important in a relationship. Ellie doesn't know how to trust because of what she has seen in her work as well as in her past. Has anyone caused you to distrust them? Why? How did you settle it?

2. Who is your favorite character? Why?

3. Ellie is self-reliant, and has to be in her job. But when she protects Winnie, she comes to depend on Colt—at first reluctantly, later because she has no choice. Do you consider yourself independent, needing no one? Is it possible to go through life not needing anyone? Ellie discovers she must depend on others at times. Who do you depend on and why?

4. How do you feel about the resolution at the end between Colt and Ellie? How would you have liked the book to end?

5. What is your favorite scene? Why?

6. Colt is torn between two jobs—working for the family business and being a marine biologist. Have you ever been torn between

doing two different jobs? How did you resolve it? Are you happy with your choice?

7. Ellie's relationship with her mother is nonexistent because of their past. She hasn't been able to forgive her mother and move beyond her anger. Do you or someone you know have a similar relationship with a parent? How have you or that parent dealt with the situation?

8. Colt couldn't forgive his father. He was neglected as a child and then his dad died without any resolution between father and son. Although he is loved by his grandparents, Colt has an emptiness inside. Is there someone in your past that has done that to you? How can you get past that?

9. Winnie's life is in danger. This is hard for Colt to handle. When life seems impossible, what do you do? Who do you turn to for help?

10. Although Ellie knew she should forgive her mother, that God wanted her to, she couldn't. Have you ever done something you know you shouldn't or avoid what you knew you should do? How did that situation turn out?

11. Who did you think was after Winnie? Why?

12. The villain was motivated by revenge. How can we get past wanting to retaliate against someone who we thought hurt us?

13. Winnie has a hard time believing someone wants to kill her. She has never intentionally hurt anyone enough to make a person want her dead. She doesn't know how to deal with it. What would you do if someone felt that kind of anger toward you?

14. Winnie felt she owed Steve Fairchild a public apology because of what happened when her husband died. Others didn't feel she did. The first opportunity she had she made the apology. Have you ever done that? How did the person react? How did you feel afterward?

15. Ellie's brother was bullied when he was alive because he was slow and different. Ellie became tough in order to protect her twin brother. Have you ever stood up to a bully to protect yourself or another? How did it turn out for you?

Get 2 Free Books,
Plus 2 Free Gifts—
just for trying the Reader Service!

Get 2 Free Books,
Plus 2 Free Gifts—
just for trying the Reader Service!

LIS17R2

Get 2 Free Books,
Plus 2 Free Gifts—
just for trying the
Reader Service!

Love Inspired HISTORICAL

LIHI7R2

Get 2 Free Books,
Plus 2 Free Gifts—
just for trying the Reader Service!

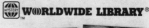

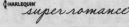